# Zion
# Gold Rush

C. R. Fulton

THE CAMPGROUND KIDS
www.bakkenbooks.com

*Zion Gold Rush* by C. R. Fulton
Revised Edition
Copyright © 2022  C.R. Fulton

Cover Credit: Anderson Design Group, Inc.

All rights reserved. This book is protected under the copyright laws of the United States of America. This book may not be copied or reprinted for commercial gain or profit.

ISBN 978-1-955657-17-4
For Worldwide Distribution
Printed in the U.S.A.

BAKKEN
BOOKS

PUBLISHED BY BAKKEN BOOKS
2022

*To my family…
we have been "glamping" full time for years now.
I wouldn't change a thing!*

**National Park Adventures: Series One**
*Grand Teton Stampede*
*Smoky Mountain Survival*
*Zion Gold Rush*
*Rocky Mountain Challenge*
*Grand Canyon Rescue*

**National Park Adventures: Series Two**
*Yellowstone Sabotage*
*Yosemite Fortune*
*Acadia Discovery*
*Glacier Vanishing*
*Arches Legend*

For more books, check out:
www.bakkenbooks.com

# - 1 -

Dad stares at his phone for a minute before he hangs up. "Well, that was certainly an interesting conversation."

My nine-year-old sister Sadie looks up from her drawing, pushing her long brown hair over one shoulder. She hasn't smiled much lately, which is weird.

Mom pulls a tray of brownies out of the oven. "Are you going to tell us about it?"

I run a hand through my short blond hair, biting my tongue with excitement. *Dad's eyes don't glint like that unless he's got big news.*

"Hmmm." He scowls at his phone, tapping away.

Mom turns to him, one hand on her hip. "So help me, I will not give you even one stevia-sweetened brownie if you don't speak up soon." Mom slaps her oven mitt playfully on the counter.

I sure am glad she found stevia; it tastes like sugar but doesn't make Sadie go wild.

A teasing grin appears on Dad's face. "You drive a hard bargain."

Mom simply raises her eyebrows.

"Right. So, that was the St. George Dinosaur Discovery Site."

*That is interesting.*

"Annnddd?" Mom asks, holding the brownies hostage.

"They would like me to come out to scan and 3D print some of their new dinosaur fossils that haven't even been classified yet."

"Where is it?" I ask, my head already filled with hopes.

Dad's grin grows wider. "It just so happens that the discovery site is only a stone's throw from Zion

## Zion Gold Rush

National Park, one of the most beautiful places on the earth."

Sadie and I gasp.

*This could mean adventure!*

"They want to fly me out next Friday."

Sadie and I deflate. *Now we won't even have Dad at home?*

"But…" he adds and then pauses for a long time to drive us all crazy. Mom scoots the tray of brownies farther behind her.

Dad squints, giving in. "One of the staff members at the museum has an RV parked at the Watchman Campground in Zion National Park, and they said we could stay in it."

"*We?*" The word squeaks out of my mouth.

"If we pay for your tickets, we could all go. What do you think, Ruth?"

Mom sniffs, pretending to be hurt. "Well, you're certainly not going without me!"

"Or us!" Sadie and I add.

"So, should I call them back with a yes?"

"Yes!"

"Wait! What about Ethan? It wouldn't seem right to go camping without him," Sadie says.

"*Glamping*, you mean," I correct her.

"What?"

"Staying in an RV is *not* camping; it's glamping—like a combination of glamorous and camping." *Still, if Dad's work gets us to Utah, I'll take it.*

"I'll call Sylvia and see what they think about Ethan coming along."

The images of the St. George Dinosaur Discovery Site are on his phone.

"I want to be a 3D printer when I grow up," I declare.

Sadie makes a face. "Well, too bad you were born a boy and not a robot."

I roll my eyes, but it's good to hear her teasing. *She seems so serious lately.*

"I don't want to *be* a printer; I want to *run* one!"

"Well, why didn't you say so?" She shakes my arm and then looks at the pictures as well. "Wow!

Real dinosaur tracks? It's so cool!" She heads off to her room. "I'll pack my sleeping bag."

"We've got to go on a plane, so almost no camping gear can come. We'll be in an RV, and it will have nearly everything we need," Dad calls after her, then turns to me. "Most of my 3D work is quite mundane, Isaiah—just creating shapes with very precise measurements on the computer. But I think you would be good at the job."

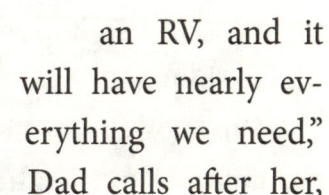

Mom sighs as she lowers her phone. "Ethan can't come. He's supposed to do a roofing job next week."

Time grinds to a sudden halt.

"No!" Sadie cries from her room. *She hears everything.* "We can't go without him."

Mom shrugs, then nibbles a brownie. I snatch two of them and head into Sadie's room. We scarf down the brownies and then get to work on the Ethan problem.

"How much money do you have?" she asks.

"Well, after I bought my compass, I have $76.27."

She releases a slow breath. "I've got $110. I don't think it will be enough to cover what the roofing job would pay."

Mom sticks her head in and comments, "It's not so much the money he would earn; it's the commitment he made to the crew. That's part of growing up. Fun things sometimes take second place to bigger commitments."

"In that case, I'll stay nine."

Sadie's comment makes Mom laugh.

*Her birthday is coming up quick, so she can't do that anyway.*

## Zion Gold Rush

"Still, the dinosaurs will be so cool."

"But Ethan loves dinosaurs."

"You mean he's terrified of them?"

The memories of Ethan's screams at Grand Teton National Park and the Smokies make us both laugh.

# -2-

"Are you excited to fly?" Sadie asks as we inch through the security line at the airport.

"Um, yeah," I answer as if she's crazy to even ask. This is our first time on a plane, and I've always dreamed of what it would be like.

"I don't want to," she mumbles. The heavy seriousness I've been noticing is back.

I tap her gently with my elbow. "What's up with you lately? I miss my bubbly, jokester sister."

Her eyes get even more sad, and she shrugs, "I don't know."

"Come on."

Her words come out in a rush. "Jenna told me

I was a mean tattletale and that she'll never be my friend again."

My jaw hangs open. "Jenna? Like the one you've hung out with since you were five?"

Sadie nods, sniffing hard. I blink rapidly, trying to absorb just how deep that threat would hurt.

"What did you tell on her about?"

"That new girl Breanna was making of fun Nell, and Jenna jumped right in with her. I told them to stop because Nell was already crying. But they wouldn't, so I told the teacher."

"And somehow that makes *you* mean? Sadie, you know you did what's right."

She makes a disbelieving face as we heft our carry-on bags onto the rollers for the airport security scanning.

"Shoes off, empty your pockets, put your items in the bin, and then step through the metal detectors." The transportation security officer shoves our bags through a screening tunnel, and we follow Mom and Dad through the archway.

I breathe a sigh of relief that Mom had double-checked to see that I hadn't packed Poppa's knife in my pocket. I had planned to leave it in the truck, and at the last minute, we had switched it to the checked bags that will ride in the plane's belly. *I feel naked without it.*

Sadie pulls her cowgirl boots back on and smiles sadly at Mom as she lifts her backpack off the far side of the conveyor.

Mom's eyes flick to mine. Even without words, we agree. *We have got to help Sadie.*

Dad hangs up his phone. "Well, that was an interesting conversation."

"Not again!" Mom, Sadie, and I say in unison as we head toward our flight's gate.

"And you all…with no hot, gooey brownies to use as leverage," Dad gloats.

"Ugh!" Sadie groans.

"I'll tell you on one condition."

We all hold our breath. *Sadie smiles, for real.*

She cocks her head and rolls her eyes, but with

all of us staring at her so intently, that familiar grin grows on one side of her mouth then spreads to the other.

"Deal. Now tell us!" she begs.

"Someone will be meeting us in Utah."

I frown. "Who?"

"Guess…" Dad says.

Sadie and I look at each other sharply. "Ethan?"

Dad nods, and we cheer. "The roofer ordered the wrong materials, and the right stuff won't be in for at least a month. Ethan's flight should land an hour after ours."

Zion National Park now seems like the perfect adventure.

# -3-

With an angled roof and large sections made of glass, the St. George Dinosaur Discovery Site building looks cool.

"Scel...Scelidosaurus? The only one of its kind in America?" Sadie reads the big sign on the side of the wall.

"Wow!" Ethan's voice is full of the awe that I feel as we step into the site. Huge rocks full of dinosaur footprints stand upright throughout half of the building. The other half has a walkway built over the actual ground punctured with hundreds of dinosaur tracks.

Dad shakes hands with a staff member named

## Zion Gold Rush

Dixie, and we get to step behind the scenes into a large room labeled "Staff Only" where people are studying rocks.

Dad sets down his scanner, and Dixie turns to us. "Would you kids like a guided tour?"

"No way!" Ethan is over the top. "Dinosaurs actually walked *right here!*"

The lifelike statues right next to the footprints send chills across my skin. *It sure feels like one could run through here any second. But now I'm being like Ethan.*

Dixie points to a spot where a herd had passed by. "These are called Grallator tracks. If you know some about dinosaurs, you might know that there isn't a dinosaur called a Grallator. That's because the tracks are named differently from the creatures that made them. Determining exactly which species made the print is really difficult, so it's easier to give the prints their own name."

I think the most amazing exhibit in the entire building is the place where a dinosaur had laid on the lakeshore with its front feet curled up just like our hands would be when we sleep.

"Marcy can give you the keys to the RV if you're ready."

Mom and Dad nod at Dixie's comment.

"We would love for you to get started with the scans this afternoon..." Dixie continued, "if you think you can get settled by then."

"No problem," Dad answers.

My head is full of dinosaur facts as we drive into Zion National Park. One thing's for sure, I've never seen a place that looks more like it should have living dinosaurs walking around in it. The sheer red and gold cliffs rise skyward, and the lush green valleys are breathtaking.

We jump out at the huge park sign and line up for the picture. I throw my arm around Sadie, making a funny face to make her laugh.

"Three, two, one..."

"Pterodactyl!" I shout, pointing to a huge, winged shape cruising between the canyon walls. Of course, it passed over just in time for me to look ridiculous in the picture.

"Thanks, *Ethan*." Sadie elbows me, and I smile sheepishly.

"Actually, *young Sir*," Ethan says in the deep voice of a radio announcer, "the creature you're referring to appears to be a golden eagle." We pile back into the car.

"Wow!" Mom says, leaning over the dash of the rental car for a better look.

*There's just something special about Zion…it's as if we're being sucked back in time where anything could happen.*

Dad turns in to the Watchman Campground. "Our RV should be in spot number six on row two."

We smash our noses into the window, leaning over to count the sites.

"It's huge!" Sadie squeaks as we turn in next to a huge fifth-wheel camper. "And I must admit, it looks pretty cool!"

"Take your shoes off at the door!" Mom calls as

we make a mad dash to look inside. Ethan wins the race with his longer legs, but there's a pile up on the metal stairs. Dad reaches over our heads to unlock the door. Ducking under Ethan's arm, Sadie shoots inside first!

"It has a bunk loft!" she cries as I finally get in the door. The kitchen is straight ahead, with a couch to the left.

"I call the loft!" I shout as I stare up at the bed that's tucked up against the ceiling. *Maybe glamping won't be that bad after all.*

"Um... How does the toilet work?" Sadie calls from the bathroom.

I leap up the two stairs, leading to the bedroom and bathroom. "You flush it, of course..." I frown over her shoulder at the strange pedal on the floor next to the toilet. "Oh..."

Sadie's mouth makes a flat line as she blinks at me. "See?"

"Okay," Dad says, squeezing into the tiny space with us. "You push the pedal halfway to fill the toilet

## Zion Gold Rush

with water. After you finish, push the pedal all the way down to flush."

I test out the pedal, and sure enough, water rushes in when I push it.

"All right! Out with you all, please," Sadie begs, nearly dancing in place.

Dad and I head back to the kitchen. I'm about to climb up to the loft when Dad says, "Isaiah, help me bring in the bags. Then I've got to get back to work."

"Sure thing, Dad." All I want to do is climb the ladder to the loft, but Mom smiles at me for my good attitude as I turn to help Dad.

# -4-

By the time we set up our belongings in the RV, it's midafternoon. *I can't wait to explore Zion!*

"Mom, how far is it to a hiking place?" Sadie asks, but I can still see the heaviness in her eyes from Jenna's hurtful words. *Maybe this trip will help her forget.*

"I think it's a five-minute hike from here to the Zion Canyon Visitor Center. There, we need to board a shuttle bus to take us into the rest of the park."

"But how do we get back?" Ethan asks around a mouthful of cookie.

"The same way. I've read that the wait for a shuttle can be long if there's a crowd. But we can

## Zion Gold Rush

walk to the shuttle from this campground. Here's some snacks we can take with us."

Stretching my legs after the long day of travel feels so good as we pack our things. Having Poppa's knife back in my pocket feels even better.

"Hey!" Ethan says as we near the visitor center. "There was this dinosaur who sold shirts. What did she name her business?"

I roll my eyes and then scan the incredible cliff faces all around us. They tower up in shades of red and gold, and the scrubby trees all around seem like they could conceal any kind of creature.

"Dino shirts?" Sadie says with her nose wrinkled on one side.

"Try *Sarah's Tops!*" Ethan slaps his leg as he laughs.

Mom sucks in a sharp breath.

"What?" I ask, searching for wolves or bears, my hair standing on end.

"Ethan," she says seriously. "Are you now taller than me?"

With a wide grin, Ethan steps up to Mom. "Aunt Ruth. I can now look down on you."

It's true. Ethan is tall, and his lean frame puts his nose level with Mom's eyes. "But, for the record, I'll always look up to you." He cracks up again as we enter the crowded visitor center. Ethan selects a small pickax and steps in line to buy it.

Mom asks for three sets of Junior Ranger booklets. "Oh, and do we need tickets to ride the shuttle system?" she asks the ranger, whose name tag says Rob.

"Nope, as of last year, we switched to a free ride system," Rob says with a wide smile. "You all be careful and monitor the weather. Flash floods are the most dangerous part of Zion. If rain is in the forecast, don't hike in any of the lower canyons. The water can rise faster than you could ever imagine. Oh, and the shuttles run daily from 6:00 a.m. to 5:00 p.m." He checks his watch. "You'll have time to hike the west bank of the Virgin River if you're heading out now."

## Zion Gold Rush

"Great info, thank you," Mom says, and we hurry out of the bright visitor center.

Three shuttles fill up before the line inches forward enough for us to board one.

"Mom, I want to sit with you." Sadie takes Mom's hand in the crowd. Most of the seats are already full. Ethan swings into an empty bench, but before I can slide in with him, a man with a bushy beard and the biggest hiker's backpack I've ever seen takes the space.

I frown, nabbing a seat next to an Asian man who's chattering on his phone in a strange language. Mom and Sadie slide in behind me, and I watch the man next to Ethan try to stay in the seat. His pack must be heavy because he's having trouble adjusting it.

Ethan looks over his shoulder at me, making a funny face. I look back at Ethan's seat companion. His pack is so big, it almost takes up the entire seat, leaving his bottom hanging over into the aisle. The man's knees, which are pressed against the seat in front of him, seems to be what is keeping him in the seat.

The shuttle lurches forward, and the views make my mouth hang open in awe. People flow on and off the shuttle at the next three stops.

The man next to Ethan struggles to get off the bench at Stop 5. He tries twice before he can lurch off the seat with his heavy pack. I slip between people to take the seat next to Ethan.

He's frowning at the space the man had vacated. "Wait, don't sit down," Ethan says, brushing strange black dust from the seat.

"What is that?" I ask.

Ethan is creating a small dust cloud. "I'm not sure." He sniffs his hand and makes a sour face. "Stinks, whatever it is."

"Pulling forward. All passengers must be seated!" The driver, with heavy brows and a thick lower lip, frowns at me in the large rearview mirror. I plop down onto Ethan's fingers.

"Ouch!" The bus lurches forward. "I need those

fingers to eat my duplex cookies. You should be more careful."

"Duplex?" I question.

"Yeah." He pulls one out of his bag. "A duplex is a multilevel building. Look at this here cookie. See all the beautiful levels? Butter cookie on the bottom, creamy filling, and on top, an intricately stamped roof." He stuffs the entire cookie into his mouth and starts singing, blowing a crumb or two out with his song. "Duplex cookies, sittin' on my shelf. Duplex cookies, headed to my mouth."

"Oh, man," I mutter as the bus pulls forward. I catch Sadie's voice behind us.

"Mom, that sign said West Bank Trail!" I twist, watching the sign disappear.

"Oh!" Mom says, frowning at the map. "You're right; we missed our stop. We'll have to ride the whole loop and get off on the way back."

We regroup after arriving at Stop 5 the second time. Seeing the whole loop had been worth the extra riding time. The furthermost stop had been a place called the Narrows, and from what I see, I can't wait to hike it.

"Okay, let's take on the West Bank Trail!" Mom is really getting into this outdoor stuff; she's lost 15 pounds since we started hiking.

"Here, Mom, I'll carry your bag." It never hurts to butter her up while we're doing my absolute favorite thing on earth, exploring a new wilderness.

"Thanks," Mom says, squeezing my arm in a half hug, but she frowns at Sadie's serious expression. She needs to laugh a little, and I believe I know exactly how to make that happen.

"Hey, Ethan," I say as we start down the trail. "What do you get if you cross a dinosaur and a pig?"

Ethan scowls at me, chewing his lip in thought.

"Give up?"

"I will never admit defeat."

I roll my eyes and give him the answer, "Jurassic pork!"

"That's actually a funny one, Rawlings. But what do you call a small group of singing dinosaurs?"

"A choir?" Sadie guesses.

"No, a Tyranno-chorus!" Ethan cackles at his own joke so hard even Sadie cracks a smile.

"Hey," she says, shielding her eyes from the lowering sun. "What's that guy doing?"

I squint across the plain before us with a creek running through the center. Against the red-and-cream streaks of the sheer cliff wall, a man is carefully studying the rocks.

"Isn't that the guy who sat next to you, Ethan?" Sadie asks.

"Naw. Wait. Yeah, it is. Look at his huge pack. He can hardly stand up."

"Is there a trail out that way?" Sadie slides the map from Mom's back pocket. She frowns at it for a moment, tracing it with her finger.

"No, the only trail is this one."

The man stomps off, and right before our eyes, he disappears into the cliff face!

# -5-

"Where did he go?" I ask in amazement.

"Mom, can we investigate?" Sadie pulls at Mom's elbow.

"Oh, I don't know; we better not miss the last shuttle." She looks down at Sadie, noticing her eyes are bright for the first time in far too long. "But I guess we could hike over there and skip the rest of the trail."

"Yesss!" Sadie jumps high, then sets off through the cottonwood trees. Two steps later, I discover that what I thought was sagebrush is thorn bushes!

"Ugh! Ouch!" Ethan cries. He's found them too.

"Come on, this way." Sadie nimbly slips around

## Zion Gold Rush

the creek while Ethan and I try to escape the painful grip of the vines.

"The...things I...willingly do for my sister!" I yank free of the last of them and instantly regret it. My arm is bleeding. We splash across the creek as I wipe it off.

"Oh! Ouch! I guess it's my turn." Mom twists, vines sticking to her shorts. A few feet later, we're among huge boulders strewn at the base of the cliff.

"Listen, kids. I've got a pebble in my shoe. Stay within sight, all right?"

"Sure, Mom!" I agree, squinting up at the cliffs straight ahead. Sadie's excitement is rubbing off on me. We leave Mom pulling off her shoe.

"Wow! I knew it!" Sadie says, reaching out to touch a cliff. "I knew he was looking at something!"

"What is it?" I question, stepping closer. I see a strange set of markings on the rock.

"Looks like ancient Indian lettering to me," Ethan comments, his hands resting on his hips.

As I study the etching, my interest grows. "Maybe this is from Native Americans."

"What?" Sadie cries. "Native Americans drew pictures! These are English letters and numbers; it's just that they don't make sense."

Ethan leans forward. "Excellent deduction, Sherlock."

"Thanks," Sadie replies dryly.

"How old do you think this writing is?" I ask, wondering who had scraped the letters and numbers into the rock. *Maybe a warrior or an outlaw hiding from a posse left the puzzling message.*

"I don't know..." Sadie whispers.

"10N 25F 5B 11N 7S 3D," I read, my curiosity growing.

"Hey, I wonder..." Ethan says, rummaging in his pack. "Oh, a cookie!" he says delightedly as he pops the entire thing into his mouth and mumbles some unintelligible words. Pulling out the pickax he had bought at the visitor center, he raises it high.

"No!" Sadie and I yell together, but our words

fail to prevent him from hammering the pick into the cliff right above the writing.

A cracking sound like ice breaking up echoes, and a segment of rock slides down and hits the ground with a dull thud.

"Ethan!" Sadie rushes forward to flip over the slab. "Oh, no, you broke it!" She holds up the last two letters on a small piece of rock that had split from the rest.

"Oops." A red flush creeps up Ethan's neck. "Well…I didn't expect that to…you know…work."

The main slab is heavy in my hands. "Well, I don't think we should just leave it here. It'll fit inside my pack."

Sadie hands the smaller piece to Ethan, who holds it up to the bigger slab. "At least nothing was lost. I wonder what the letters and numbers could mean."

"Come on, kids!" Mom calls. "We've got a shuttle to catch." Mom straightens from emptying her boot near the boulders.

"Well, Ethan. It only took you all of five seconds to dislodge a priceless artifact."

"Yep. That's true. My new pick allows me to do stupid things faster!" The red on Ethan's cheeks grows a shade darker. Looking down, he fingers the small pickax.

We hurry back to the shuttle stop and sit on some rocks at the edge of a large group of people also waiting.

"Mom, what if there is no room on the last shuttle?" I ask.

"They won't leave anybody out here overnight. Don't worry."

I watch Ethan open his bag of trail mix.

"Aw!" Sadie croons. "Look, a chipmunk!"

"Actually, it's three."

They skitter from under the rocks with soft brown eyes. Their fur is streaked white, brown and gold.

Ethan holds out a peanut to the chipmunk, but Mom says, "Remember, Ethan, we can never feed wildlife in a national park—no matter how cute they are."

"Sorry, little guy. Rules are rules." Ethan pops the nut into his mouth just before the first chipmunk can grab it. Chirping disgustedly, the chipmunk stands on its hind legs.

"They are so adorable!" Sadie is lying on her stomach, studying them.

"Great! Now all we're going to hear is 'I want a chipmunk.'" I say, but my annoyance is fake. *I'm so glad Sadie is enjoying today.*

The chipmunk that almost had Ethan's nut chirps and clucks rapidly, and the other two snap to attention. Together, they advance on Ethan, their tiny bellies low to the ground.

"Um, Ethan? I think you made them angry," I say, watching more chipmunks emerge from under the rocks. They run to Sadie and climb into her open hand and scurry over her back.

"Look!" she whispers, completely in love with the little creatures.

Ethan has one an inch from his leg.

"Sorry, guys. I'm not allowed to feed you." He stuffs a handful of trail mix into his mouth. The first one chirps, and all the chipmunks leap onto Ethan's leg.

"Eh! Take it easy, Chippys. Go away!" Ethan squirms, but the creatures prove impossible to dislodge. They streak up his chest and race down his arms. "Help! They're…ehhh!"

The leader of the chipmunk army leaps for his snack bag, which is hanging open as he struggles to be free of the others.

"They tickle. Oh! Ouch! They're scratching me." He's flat on the ground now, and the chipmunk lands in the bag of trail mix like a high diver with perfect form. Disappearing for a second, its head pops up, cheeks now stuffed with food.

Ethan flings his arm, and trail mix explodes everywhere. The chipmunk somersaults out of the bag and lands on the run, a triumphant look in his beady little eyes.

## Zion Gold Rush

In seconds, an entire army of chipmunks appears, gathering up Ethan's spill.

"Don't feed them, Ethan!" Mom cries, turning from studying the map. It's chipmunk chaos as their brown-and-white striped bodies rush everywhere. In three breaths, no trace of Ethan's trail mix is left anywhere on the ground!

Ethan holds up his empty bag. "Hey, I was going to eat that!"

Sadie giggles. "I think you made them angry, offering that nut and then eating it instead."

"I have to admit, they are super cute with their cheek pouches all stuffed full!"

"The bus is here!" Mom calls. I pull Ethan up from the ground, and we climb the big square steps with the same heavy featured driver. As I walk by, I catch his name tag—*Floyd.*

# -6-

"Mom, can we explore until you're ready?" I ask as she packs Dad a lunch the next day.

"Sure...but please stay within sight of the campground."

"Sweet! Come on."

Ethan, Sadie and I head to the right of the visitor center. "Is there a valley this way?"

It's like a mini-Zion canyon, but instead of 1500-foot-high cliffs, these are 10-to-15 feet high.

"This looks like the perfect place for a Dilophosaurus to make a nest," Ethan says, his eyes darting around nervously.

"Take it easy! They're extinct, remember?" I say.

## Zion Gold Rush

"It sure doesn't seem like it—at least not here—not with their footprints on those very cliffs." Ethan points at the canyon.

"What? There are Dino prints in the park too?" Sadie asks.

"Yep. I read about it at the Dinosaur Site. The prints in Zion are extremely hard to get to, and they're in an unsafe place for the public. So the park rangers won't tell where they are." He scans the valley ahead through the cottonwood trees. "It could be right up there."

"That isn't high or dangerous," Sadie says flatly.

Ethan shrugs. "Anything could happen on this trip."

"Oh, boy." I roll my eyes. "I think we've had enough excitement already with the bears and the skunk when we went camping in the Smokies."

"What's that?" Ethan's harsh whisper makes me drop to one knee next to him. Talking about bears has me on edge.

"Right there…the brown and white. See it?"

A jolt of adrenaline hits me as I spot the out-of-place color.

"Could be a bighorn sheep," I whisper.

Sadie is the only one still standing in the open. "It's not an animal," she declares.

"How do you know?"

"Because it's not. Trust me, I know animals, and that isn't one." She strides forward.

"Sadie, wait!" Ethan whispers, "It could be a Bambiraptor!"

She spins, her mouth flat in disdain of our cowardice. "Come on, boys."

I hop up, breaking free of Ethan's case of nerves. After all, there's no sensation in my chest as if danger is near. "You're right," I say, hurrying to catch up to Sadie.

"It's garbage!" she says. "Why do people litter? What is wrong with leaving things better than you found them?"

The pile is as high as my hips, and it seems to be composed of one type of packaging.

"Dyno..." Ethan steps up and tries to read the print on the cardboard. "Dyno...Nobel."

"Do you think someone found dinosaur bones and is going to cast them?" Sadie asks.

Ethan frowns. "I suppose you could sell a dinosaur bone for a lot of money. But surely it would be illegal to steal ancient artifacts from a national park."

"Yeah." Sadie crosses her arms. "Just watch out when you tell someone that they're doing something wrong. It might not be worth it."

I frown at the sad expression in her eyes, hating how Jenna's words are becoming a part of her. Every day they steal from her. *It's just not right, especially when Jenna was the one doing wrong.*

"Listen, if someone is taking things from a national park, it's our job as junior rangers to stop them. Explore. Learn. Protect. That is Zion's Junior Ranger motto, so first, we must get all this trash off the ground."

We cram the thin cardboard into three almost

manageable piles. But no matter how hard Ethan tries, he can't get his last piece to stay in his arms. As soon as he awkwardly bends to pick it up, another piece falls out the back.

Sadie sighs, snatching it from him. "My arms are like twice as short as yours! And I can carry more than you?"

I can tell she's pleased that she can.

"I do have super long arms, but you are using your chin too!" Ethan's defense falls flat as another piece flops to the ground next to him.

"Maybe you should try it," Sadie says dryly. "Besides what happened to Ninja Ethan, who snatched every shred of garbage in the Smokies?"

"Ugh!" Ethan bends awkwardly to grab the piece. "That skunk at the Smoky Mountains killed him." He lowers his chin onto his stack. "Oh. That does help."

"Let's put it in the dumpsters behind the visitor center," I say, grappling with the strange-smelling trash.

## Zion Gold Rush

By the time we're heaving it into the dumpsters, it occurs to me that we're far from the RV. "Oh, no! Mom said to stay in sight!"

"We better run!" Sadie takes off down the path, heading back to the Watchman Campground.

We round the bend, and sweat is dripping when I hear Mom's distant voice calling us.

"Coming," I call, but I'm breathing too hard to create much volume. By the time we reach the camper, I need to brace my hands on my knees for support.

"Sorry, Mom!" Sadie pants.

"Did you see a dinosaur or something?" Mom asks, eyeing us and wondering why we're breathing so hard.

"No. But we found quite a pile of garbage." Ethan holds up one hand. Grimacing, his other hand is on his side as if it hurts. "Not to worry, Aunt Ruth. We conquered it."

"Taking care of the garbage caused us to get out of your sight. Sorry, Mom, that was wrong," I add.

"Well, I appreciate your honesty. Be more careful about obeying next time, okay?"

"Yeah."

"How about a popsicle?" she asks. I had seen her put a box of stevia-sweetened treats in the freezer. I sure am glad stevia is getting so popular. It's opened a whole new world of desserts for our family.

"Maybe glamping does have its perks," I admit. "It sure is nice to have a freezer."

"I could get used to it," Mom says.

"But, Mom, it's nothing like a tent! In here, you're all closed off from nature."

"Right. With a toilet so you don't have to take a midnight walk, and…a freezer for popsicles."

"Mooomm."

"I know you love your tent camping, but you have to admit, I've been quite a trooper on all our adventures. Just let me enjoy this one, and I'll be ready for the tent next time."

The frosty popsicle sticks to my lips. By the

time we walk to the shuttle stop next to the visitor center, I'm slurping up the last of my strawberry goodness.

"I wonder when they'll make Stevia marshmallows..." Sadie considers as we join the crush of people, trying to fit through the shuttle door.

I elbow Ethan. His riding buddy from last time is straight ahead of us. This time his huge pack looks just as heavy as before. *I'm not going to be surprised if it tips him over any second.* But it's kind of odd-shaped—as if a pipe is trying to poke out both ends.

We end up sitting right behind him. Ethan, never too good at being discreet, snaps his fingers. "That's where I recognize that smell from."

# - 7 -

The man turns to scowl at us. I widen my eyes and shrink into the seat. *I don't trust something about him.* I give Ethan an annoyed look when the man turns back around.

Today, we hike a part of the Narrows. This trek winds between towering cliffs walls as high as 1500 feet and, at its most narrow point, the entire canyon is only 22 feet wide. The description in the brochure says, for almost the entire hike, a crystal-clear creek flows at the base of the cliffs. I can't wait to soak my feet in the water.

As the shuttle slows at Stop 5, the man with the pack starts to get up before the bus has braked to

## Zion Gold Rush

a complete stop. Let me rephrase that: he tries to stand. His third effort to gain his feet finally works, and as he steps sideways down the aisle, something flutters to the floor.

Everyone is shifting, getting ready to disembark or to let someone out of the seat. Across the aisle, a woman's purse has gotten snagged under the seat, and she's blocking everyone behind her from exiting the bus.

I sit back. *This could be a long wait.* The man with the pack strides to the exit, just ahead of the jam. I watch him in the massive rearview mirror. When he passes Floyd, that tingling feeling in my chest begins. Floyd gestures at the man and whispers something.

*Packman* makes an angry face and slashes downward with his hand. He frowns at Floyd—as if he didn't want to have any words between them. Floyd flinches, glancing out the windshield as if he didn't see Packman at all.

The woman trying to get her purse is getting

desperate. As she jerks harder at the straps on her purse, I reach down to pick up the slip of paper that had fallen when Packman had stood.

Fingering the shred, I frown when I see the letter D, then half of another letter that I'm nearly certain is a Y. I elbow Ethan.

"Ow, my ribs are getting sore from your continually elbowing me."

I roll my eyes. "Look!" I hold out the paper, and his gaze snaps up to mine.

"Do you think Packman dropped it? Or do you think it might have been on his bench, and his moving knocked it off?"

I shrug. "There's no way to know for sure."

Finally, the woman's purse comes free with a shredding sound, and she groans, frowning at a ragged tear. The line to get off the bus finally starts moving.

When we get off at the Narrows, I show Sadie the shred of paper. Her mouth forms a silent O.

"I wish we could've heard what old Floyd said to that guy," Sadie says.

"You mean the driver?" Mom asks, tightening her pack.

"Yeah."

"I know what it was!" Her eyes twinkle.

"How?" Sadie questions.

"I can read lips. Remember how you guys always wondered how I knew what you were up to? Well, now you know. Anyway, he said, 'Did you find it?'"

Ethan, Sadie and I look at each other. *Something is up for sure. But we won't dare to whisper around Mom anymore.*

---

"So, Dad's not even going to be here for dinner?" I whine after our amazing hike through the Narrows.

"Well, he had the first print of the dinosaur bones started, but the printer bed was off temperature, so he had to recalibrate the machine. If he doesn't get a print started tonight, there's no way he'll get this project completed by Friday."

"So…we would get to stay longer?"

"No, he would not have fulfilled his contract."

"Aww." I slump, missing Dad.

"To make it up to you, tonight we're going to attend the Ranger-led stargazing program."

"They have that here?"

"Zion is one of the best places on earth to stargaze. And look, there's not a cloud in the sky. That will make the evening a little better, right? Plus, you can check it off in your Junior Ranger book."

"Yeah," I say. "How long until we leave?"

She checks her phone. "Fifteen minutes."

The sun is rapidly going down, and with it, the temperature is cooling from its intense heat. The rock with the letters and numbers scratched on it is still in my pack, so I lug it to the big storage area on the outside of the camper. I carefully set the slab inside and then freeze.

"Mom!" I shout.

# -8-

She's at the camper door in half a heartbeat.

"What?"

"There's a tent in here!"

"Isaiah! I thought you were hurt."

I cover a slight smirk. "Sorry, Mom. Can Ethan and I sleep in it tonight?"

"Well, maybe…."

"Me too!" Sadie says as she perks up. She's just been sitting alone at the picnic table, brooding as Jenna's words continue to eat at her.

"Sorry, Sadie. We will let the boys have the tent without you tonight."

"Bummer." She slumps again.

Mom and I frown at each other.

"You can sleep in my loft," I offer.

"Really?" Sadie turns, studying me.

"Of course. Anything for the best sister ever."

"Thanks, Bud," she says with half of a sad smile.

"Okay, let's get ready for some stargazing. Everyone, bring your sweatshirts. The temperature will keep dropping."

*Mom is right.* As we join a small crowd of people near the visitor center, I'm thankful to pull on a thick hoodie. In the half-light of dusk, I see the crisp outlines of five telescopes spread over the valley floor.

"Do you think we'll get a chance to use one, Mom?"

"The ranger said we could."

"Okay! Welcome to the Zion National Park stargazing event." A slim woman with a wide-brimmed hat motions us closer.

"I'm an astronomy ranger here at the park, and my name is Amy. Ranger Rob will also help you understand the sky tonight. While it gets good and dark for us, I will share a few facts with you. Zion is one of the top locations on earth for stargazing because of the combination of a few factors. Who can guess what they might be?"

"Your super powerful telescopes!" a man from the crowd answers.

"Nope!" Ranger Amy laughs. "Although we will enjoy using them tonight, the most important factor that will allow you to see more stars than you have ever seen before is *air quality*."

"That was my second guess," the man says.

"Sure! You might not think that factories, cars and pollution affect how you see the sky, but they do. You might have a sky completely clear of clouds, but you won't see many stars. That's because of a kind of smog that hangs in the air. Here at Zion, we have an extremely small population. Everybody, take a big deep breath of pure Utah air!"

The whole crowd does, and I find the lungful is sweet.

"That's some of the cleanest air in the United States. The next factor making Zion a prime spot to look at the stars is minimal light projection. These canyon walls block out what little light comes from Springdale and the other towns nearby."

By the time she has the first telescope set properly, I'm biting my lower lip with excitement. "Come here, young man. Do you want to look at Jupiter?" I realize Amy is looking at me.

"Me?" My voice comes out like a squeak.

"Sure! Step on up!"

I close one eye and lean in toward the black rubber ring at the bottom of the telescope, then I gasp long and loud.

"Tell us what you see," Ranger Amy invites.

"I…it's incredible! Jupiter looks like it's covered in blue clouds surrounded with bands of red!" I've never seen anything like it before.

"Can you tell us how many moons orbit the planet?"

"Um…" I start to count, but she continues.

"Just kidding! That would take a long time; Jupiter has 79 moons!"

"Can my sister look next?" I ask.

"Sure thing," Ranger Amy replies.

I pull Sadie up to the telescope. The awe of seeing the planet with my own eyes still grips me with wonder.

"Oh!" she cries in astonishment.

"Maybe I'll be an astronomer instead of a 3D printer."

"A 3D printer operator," Sadie corrects me, her eye still pressed against the telescope.

"What are those clouds that are rising over the cliffs?" Ethan asks, pointing to a bright smudge in the sky.

"Ah!" Ranger Amy sighs fondly. "That's not a cloud. It's the Milky Way, the galaxy that includes our solar system. I never get tired of seeing it rise. Did you know less than a third of Americans can see the Milky Way from where they live? Just look at all of those stars!"

Time flies as we fall in love with the night sky. Most of us end up lying on our backs, just soaking in the beauty of the sky above us.

Ranger Rob stands nearby, and another visitor asks, "Sir, what's your favorite legend about Zion?"

Rob sucks in a breath, thinking hard. "It would have to be the legend of the White Cliffs Lost Gold Mine. The legend says in 1870 a young man named Hubbell heard about a cave here in Zion that was filled with quartz icicles covered with veins of gold. Determined to find the cave, he traveled from Mexico to Utah. His instructions said to look for a V-shaped crevice in a cliff. At the bottom of the V would be a jumble of boulders that made the passage seem like a dead end. He was told to look for a stream flowing from a small entrance.

Hubbell searched for weeks near Deer Springs Wash with no luck. Giving up the search, he returned home and set up a trading business. Thirty years later, he met Warren Peters, who was willing to take up the search. Hubbell gave him the

## Zion Gold Rush

necessary supplies, and, within a week of scouting, Peters found the gold. He could literally pick it off the huge crystals.

Peters was shocked by the amount of money the first two bags brought. Returning to Deer Springs Wash, he turned up the small canyon. But much to his dismay, he could never again find the entrance despite having drawn a map for himself. Some say local cowboys closed off the entrance to keep miners from taking over their range."

Listening to the story and looking at the sky, I can see it all happening in my mind. My fingers tingle, wondering if all that gold is still somewhere close.

"Hey," a familiar voice says.

"Dad!" I leap up and do my best to crush him in a hug.

"You all were hard to find!"

I smile up at him. "Come and look at Jupiter, Dad. It's amazing!"

# -9-

"What if that garbage was actually important evidence?" I suddenly say to Ethan and Sadie at the picnic table.

Sadie crunches some cereal. "Evidence of what? That some people are terrible at picking up after themselves?"

"No. Something bigger. Serious. Stealing dinosaur bones is illegal. I asked Mom, and she looked it up. Keeping any rocks you find inside the boundaries of a national park, especially dinosaur bones, is illegal."

We all look at each other, thinking of the code rock. "Well, I guess we had better return that to the rangers. Telling them why we have it will be embarrassing." Ethan chews on his lower lip. "But you're right. It's not like that huge pile of garbage is someone's hiking mess. They smuggled the Dyno Nobel boxes and whatever was in them into the park somehow...*and for some reason.*"

I nod. "And that means one thing..." I let the silence grow heavy, then add, "We need to get that trash back."

"Out of the dumpsters?" Sadie stands up, shocked. "I nearly puked at the smell when we put it in there!"

"Right. But without it, we'll be missing an important piece of evidence." A thought hits me. "What if the dumpsters have already been emptied?"

"We've got to hurry." Ethan stands up quickly.

"Wait, we should bring some bags to put it in. I'll get some from the camper and ask Mom if we can go to the visitor center."

Minutes later we're taking the easy walk, far outpacing Mom.

"What will we do with it? It's not like anybody's going to leave three huge bags of garbage lying around. Taking it to the Rangers wouldn't do much good without more evidence. They'll just say it's garbage." *Sadie is right, but that tingle in my chest tells me this is something we must do.*

"We'll have to hide it somewhere. If by the time we leave, we don't have any more evidence, we can turn it into the rangers."

The cool air of the visitor center is a relief. Mom waves to Ranger Rob and asks some questions about the Narrows. He extends a hand toward an elderly man with bright-blue eyes. "This is Mr. Carson. His family has been connected to Zion Canyon for over 200 years. What can you tell her about the Narrows, Mr. Carson?"

The man is obviously ancient, but he's steady and strong. "Well, my great-great-grandpappy was the first one to show Zion to the world. He painted the canyons and took the landscapes to the 1904 World's Fair in St. Louis. People refused to believe that he had painted a real place, saying he had made up the content of his paintings. But that art exhibition at the World's Fair was the catalyst to start people traveling to Zion." He clears his throat. "But you wanted to know about the Narrows…"

Not listening anymore, I peer out the back door. I nod at Ethan and Sadie, then tug at Mom's elbow. "Excuse me? Mom, can we go to the back parking lot? I can see a cool car out there!"

"All right, but don't go far and stay together."

We push through the door, and Sadie gasps, pointing toward a garbage truck pulling through the park entrance. "Oh no!"

We race toward the three dumpsters. Ethan shouts, "I'm going in!"

"What?" Sadie shrieks.

Ethan's long legs pump as he sprints toward the dumpster. Stretching high, he catches the open top, twists hard and disappears inside with a thud.

"Oh, gross!" Sadie whispers.

"We've got bigger issues than gross! How do we

stop that guy?" We both flinch as the garbage truck blasts out a piercing warning as it noses up close to the dumpster on the right. Its hydraulically controlled forks slide into the hook lift bars. The whole truck rocks as the forks lift the dumpster over the top of the cab and turn it upside down.

Sadie's fingernails dig into my arm as we watch the garbage plummet into the open truck hopper. I envision Ethan flailing through the air when the truck empties the far left dumpster. Sadie sucks in a horrified breath as the moving wall inside the hopper pushes the trash to the back of the truck.

With a bang, the lid flops closed, and the driver leans forward, watching as he lowers the empty bin back in place. The warning beep continues as he backs up and shoves the forks into the hook lift bars of the middle dumpster.

"Guysssss!" Ethan's shout is muffled. "You gotta buy me some time!"

The middle bin is in midair, and my heart rate far outpaces the awful beeping of the truck.

"Isaiah!" Sadie shaking my arm, terror in her eyes. "What do we do?"

The truck reverses and pulls up to Ethan's dumpster. I rush forward as if I'd been shot from a cannon.

"Wait!" I shout, waving my arms as I rush to the driver's door. But he can't hear me over the engine noise and the loud beeper.

"Isaiah!" Sadie yells, her hands over her mouth as she jumps in place.

*There's no more time!* In desperation, I smack the driver's door with the flat of my hand. The man jumps, then rolls down his window.

"What?" He shouts over the noise in a heavy Latino accent.

"Um, Sir, I think the end dumpster is empty enough."

He wrinkles his nose, trying to understand. "Empty?" he questions.

I nod emphatically.

"Yes, I empty. Stand back now," the man orders.

"NO! No, I mean *don't* empty it!" *Maybe that will be easier for him to understand.*

Frowning, he points at the dumpster. "Yes, I must empty."

I grab my head with both hands. "Do it next time!" I shout, sweat running between my shoulder blades.

He waves me away. "Go back. I work." He nudges the truck an inch closer.

The truth is the only option left.

"STOP!" I scream. "My cousin is in there!"

The man looks at me. "In there?" He points to the dark-green dumpster.

"Yes!" I shout, clutching the front of my shirt.

"*Uno momento.*" I watch him reach for something inside the truck. He's frowning deeply at a tiny book. I can just make out the words *Spanish to English Dictionary*. He squints, muttering, "*Cuisine…Cuisine.*"

At least I think that's what he's saying.

His mouth opens in shock as his finger stops on

the page. A sorrowful expression fills his face. "Ju *cuisine* in there?"

"What?" I shout over the roar of the engine.

He points at the book. "*Cuisine. Food.*" He motions with his hand as if he's putting food in his mouth. Then he shakes his head sadly. "Here," he twists, then turns back to me with a few dollars. "Ju take. Buy food. Not eat from dumpster."

I put my hands on my head again, "NO! My *cousin*—not *cuisine!*" I must make him understand. I grimace. "My brother. My *brother* is in there!" I point at the dumpster, and a big black bag of garbage soars out of the top.

The driver's face goes slack, his mouth open. "Brother? A *chico*?"

Another bag sails out, then the third. Two smudged hands grip the top rail, Ethan's elbow inches over it, and then his head and shoulders appear. Eyeballs bulging, he sucks in a giant breath of fresh air, then he swings over onto the pavement.

"*Chico*," the man says.

Sadie and I rush forward, grabbing the bags. She pinches her nose. "Ugh!"

I skid to a stop, waving one hand in front of my face. "Ethan..." I blink at him. I spot half a burger smashed into his hair, and a chunk of eggshell is perched on his shoulder.

"I think I might puke," Sadie says. Her voice sounds funny from pinching her nose.

"You think that's bad? How do you think I feel?"

"We've got to hurry. Mom will call any minute." I pick up a bag of garbage, and we start for the woods.

"Aye!" The driver's shout makes me spin. "*Uno?* Um...one, only one?"

"One what?" I shrug as I shout.

"One *chico*?" He points at the dumpster, his eyes wide.

"Oh! Yes, *uno!*" I hold up one finger, then give him a thumbs up. I sprint to catch up with Ethan and Sadie as I hear the dumpster slam open. The smell coming from Ethan makes me gag.

## Zion Gold Rush

"Here, let's tuck them beside this boulder and cover them up with pine needles and dirt," Sadie suggests.

We get the job done quickly, and Sadie says, "Ethan, you might want to brush your hair back a bit."

He does, and his fingers find the soggy bun. "Thought that side of my head felt a little heavy."

We rush back to the parking lot, and I take a second to admire the incredible blue Dodge Challenger. It's different than any I've seen with unique lines and different-shaped taillights. We burst through the door to find Mom just stepping away from Ranger Rob and Mr. Carson.

Ranger Rob smiles at me. "Do you like that car? I just bought it. It's a limited-make run. Only ten in the entire world are like it." He sighs, his gaze distant. "I never felt the way I did when I paid cash for that beauty, and she became mine." Then Ranger Dan makes a sour face and turns his head, sniffing. Mom covers her nose. "What is that smell?"

One side of Ethan's mouth pulls back as he crosses his arms. He, Sadie and I look at each other, our mouths clamped shut. Other shoppers in the visitor center veer out of our way.

"Ethan, it's you, isn't it?" Mom asks.

"I'll get a shower right away."

"I'm not sure that's going to cut it," she declares, one hand over her nose.

Ethan sighs. "I vowed never to bathe in tomato juice again. So I guess water will have to do."

## - 10 -

"Ha-ha!" Sadie giggles, looking at her Junior Ranger book.

"What?" I ask, sitting at the picnic table, crunching on an apple.

"Well, we have to do all the pages with Tara Tarantula and Lewis Lizard in order to become Junior Rangers. Page 5, with Tara on it, is called *Keeping the Scene Clean.*" She taps the page. "We have to list five pieces of litter that we picked up and then indicate whether or not we recycled it." She mimes with her hands and puts on an official sounding voice, "No, sir. We did not recycle it. In fact, we fished it back out of the garbage receptacle and hid it in the woods." We fall silent as Mom steps out of the RV.

"Dad is ready for me to pick him up. Do you guys want to stay here with Ethan? I shouldn't be long."

"Sure, Mom," we say in unison.

Ethan steps out of the door, his hair wet from his third shower. He smells better—a little.

Mom hugs us, then pulls out in the rental car.

"Let's make Mom and Dad dinner for a surprise," Sadie suggests.

As a rule, I don't like cooking, but I see a sparkle in Sadie's eye, so I shrug. "Okay. What should we make?"

"Mom has some ground beef that's thawed in the sink. We can make spaghetti; that's easy."

Ethan pops another of his seemingly endless stash of duplex cookies into his mouth. "I'm in. What will we make for a side dish?"

"I saw some green beans in the freezer. How about that?" A smile is turning her mouth in the right direction.

## Zion Gold Rush

Seeing her brighten visibly makes me feel good inside. "Lead on, Chef. Give me a job to do."

"Isaiah, find the biggest pot in the camper. Fill it with water and start it boiling. Ethan, hunt down some spaghetti sauce in the cupboard. I think I saw some there, and I will cook the meat."

Turns out, finding a pot and filling it are the easy part. "How on earth do we work this stove?" I ask after turning the knobs with no results.

"Mom said it's propane." Sadie's happy to know something about it.

"Okay, but how do I light it?" I ask.

Sadie puckers her lips, frowning. "That…remains a mystery."

"Well, this dinner is going nowhere fast if we don't figure it out."

Ethan pulls his head and shoulders out of the cupboard, "Aha!" He holds up a jar of spaghetti sauce. "And Ethan conquers again! So, what's the trouble?"

"We can't light the stove."

"Have no fear, Ethan's here! Step aside, young ones, and I will take care of it."

Sadie asks, "Have you ever done that before?"

"No, ma'am, I haven't, but I'm not afraid of new challenges."

"Great..." Sadie and I retreat to the far side of the couch and watch. Ethan mumbles as he reads the instructions printed on the inside of the stove cover.

"Turn knob to light." He does, and we step back again. "Use long-reach lighter to strike a flame. Hmmm." He searches around for the tool.

"It's there—hanging on the back wall." Sadie points, and Ethan grabs the lighter.

"Perfect! Okay, I'll just push this with my thumb, and I pull this trigger..." Instantly, a huge ball of flame engulfs the stovetop, flashing brightly for half a second. I hit the floor with my hands covering my head. Sadie screams loud enough for the rangers to hear at the visitor center. I look up to see Ethan standing statue-like with a shocked expression on his face.

"Are you all right?" I shout, rushing up to him.

He drops the lighter, still otherwise frozen. He looks fine, except for maybe his eyebrows, which are sort of…gray and curly. The front burner on the stove has a merry little flame burning on it.

"I vote…we just use one burner," he suggests.

"Sounds good."

Sadie reaches up and brushes Ethan's weird-looking eyebrow. The tip of each hair disintegrates.

"Good thing the flash only lasted a split second," Ethan says as he wipes his face, and the other eyebrow shortens as well. I'm relieved the camper has no damage. The only evidence of our near catastrophe is the strong smell of singed hair coming from Ethan. The singed hair smell mixes with the remaining garbage scent in a bad way.

"I'm going to get *another* shower."

Sadie and I nod at him.

"Put the noodles on first; the meat will only take a few minutes," she says.

I lift the pot of water onto the flame.

"Come on," I heard Sadie say.

I turn to see she's struggling to open the jar of spaghetti sauce.

"Here, I'll get that." I take the jar and easily pop off the lid.

"Thanks."

We both frown at a weird sound. "What…?" I whisper.

# - 11 -

I realize the burbling sound is coming from the small kitchen sink. We both lean over it, peering down the drain.

A big bubble forms, and when it pops, we both flinch. Water quickly surges into the sink from the drain.

"I'm pretty sure that's not supposed to happen," I whisper.

I hear Ethan shut off the shower, and the water goes back down a bit with a gurgle.

"Okay. That's better. It's time for the noodles," Sadie says.

I empty the package into the water and put the

lid on tight. "Okay, the package says eight minutes until they're done."

Ethan steps out of the bathroom, and I bite my lip to hold back a bark of laughter. He looks permanently surprised, with only a thin line of eyebrows left.

"I know. I know," he says, but a wet hissing sound makes us all turn.

The noodles are boiling over! A sticky yellow foam is dripping down the side of the pot and sputtering on the propane flame.

"Eh!" Sadie rushes for a hot pad, careful to lift the lid away from herself. Steam billows up in a cloud. I leap for the button on the hood and turn on the exhaust fan.

"Oh, no," Sadie says.

"What?"

"The burner went out."

Ethan sucks in a deep breath. "That is bad news. Turn off the gas!" I twist the knob, and he continues, "Are you done cooking?"

"No, the noodles aren't done, plus I need to cook the meat and the beans."

He lets out a slow breath, presses his palms together and closes his eyes for a moment. "Okay. I'm ready. Hide behind the counter."

He picks up the glass pot lid and holds it in front of his face like a shield. Then he grips the lighter with the oven mitt.

"Stay down," he says to us.

"We could go out for dinner!" I say as Sadie and I duck behind the counter. I twitch when I hear the lighter click. Heartbeats pass; nothing happens.

"Ethan?" I call.

I hear a whoosh and then see a bright light. I'm up in a flash, but Ethan is smiling. "I survived!"

Sadie takes the pot lid. "This time, let's leave the lid on crooked."

---

Later Sadie says, "The noodles are done. Here, Isaiah, please pour them into the colander."

I lean as far away from the steam as I can while

pouring out the noodles. Everything is going beautifully until that gurgling sound comes back. The cloud of steam keeps me from seeing anything.

"I think it's plugged," I announce when I see the colander, steaming water, and the noodles are floating around inside of the sink.

Sadie grabs the hot pads and snatches the colander from the sink. Ethan rushes to the bathroom, and I hear the shower door open.

"Houston, we have a problem!" he shouts, reappearing. "The shower is full too." He snaps his fingers. "Uncle Greg said he would need to dump the gray water tonight. Whatever that is."

"Well, I have to rinse the noodles, or they are going to turn into one giant blob!" Sadie says.

"Okay," I say, "Ethan, let's go dump gray water. Dad showed me where the handle is last night."

We race out the door around the back of the camper and skid to a stop next to a weird accordion-like hose that connects from the camper to a white pipe sticking up from the ground. The connection looks a little crooked, but there's no time to waste.

"Here it is!" I open a small flap and point my flashlight at the small, dark space. Three handles are lined up side-by-side.

I turn to Ethan, his nearly eyebrow-less face close, as we peer at the handles. "Which one is it?" I whisper.

"I thought you said your dad showed you the handle."

"Well, he showed me *where* they were."

"It's the middle one."

"How do you know?"

It's his turn to shrug, "I don't. Just guessing. Can you do any better?"

With a deep sigh, I reach in, my grip settling on the center handle. "Here goes nothing."

I pull hard, and the handle slides out. I hear a gurgle and then a slurp. The brown accordion hose bucks hard from the pressure and suddenly twists off the white pipe where it's connected.

Out gushes brown liquid with white flecks all over the ground.

"Eeehhhh!" Ethan leaps high into the air, screaming.

# -12-

Ethan dances away from the stinking flow. "Close it!" he screams. "That's the sewage!"

I slam the valve shut again. Ethan and I stare at the puddle of sludge and toilet paper. "Didn't know you could jump that high," I comment.

"Me neither, but no way am I going to take another shower today—especially if we can't get the gray water dumped."

"Whatever you're doing, it's not helping!" Sadie shouts from inside.

"Give me a minute!" I shout. I pull a wash hose out from the camper to spray off the accordion pipe. "Let's see. It looks like it needs to turn this way." I snap it back on to the white pipe. I hold my breath and pull the handle on the right side. The pipe bucks and gurgles, but it stays connected to the white pipe.

Sadie shouts from inside, "It's going down!"

I lean my forehead against the camper. "Whew... finally."

Ethan pulls a folding shovel from the cubby and spreads dirt over the puddle, which has long since drained into the ground.

As I look around for another shovel to help him, I notice an empty space in the storage compartment. Frowning, I question, "Hey, Ethan, did you happen to move our rock slab?"

"Nope."

I dig around some more, but it's not in the compartment anywhere. We walk back into the camper filled with the wonderful smell of food.

"Sadie, did you happen to move the code rock?"

"No, of course not. We're going to take it back to the rangers, right?"

## Zion Gold Rush

"Well, it's gone."

"Gone where?"

In frustration, I threw my hands into the air. "If I knew, I wouldn't be asking!"

"Oh, no! Not only have we lost a piece of the national park, now our fingerprints are all over the garbage! We sure look guilty." Sadie's face pales.

Ethan and I go still. *I hadn't thought of the fingerprint bit.*

"Maybe Jenna was right."

"What you mean by that?"

"Well, now it looks like we've done two illegal things. Maybe I am bad."

"Sadie, you're a wonderful person. Plus, you're the best sister ever."

"I concur," Ethan declares.

"You what?" she asks, setting full plates of food on the table.

"I agree," Ethan says.

But I can tell our words don't break through Sadie's focus on Jenna's hurtful actions.

*I wish it had never happened. Sadie didn't deserve that.* Even worse is we have now lost the code, which evidently was important enough for someone to steal.

Sadie sighs and pulls a piece of paper from her pack. "Good thing I made this...." I snatch a tracing of the rock from her hand. The sideways pencil strokes are darker on the smooth parts and lighter over the indents, showing a clear image of the code.

I grab her into a bear hug, "See? What did I tell you? You're amazing!"

The sound of car tires on gravel echoes loud. "They are here! Fill the cups, Isaiah."

Mom steps in. "Oh! You made supper!?"

We all smile tightly at her.

"Yup," I say, trying not to think about our experience with the stove and backed-up water.

Mom scowls at Ethan. "What happened to your eyebrows?"

"I...it..." He wipes a hand across his face, ending in a shrug.

## Zion Gold Rush

"Okay," she says, eyeing him. "Sadie, I'm cold, I think I'll have tea with dinner."

Our eyes go wide as Mom takes up the lighter. All three of us hit the floor, our heads covered with our hands.

Mom turns around and then gasps. "So that's what happened to your eyebrows! Listen, you always ignite the lighter first and then turn on the propane gas. I so appreciate the dinner, but I don't want any of you using the stove again."

We all nod as Dad steps inside and finds us on the floor. "What on earth is going on?"

"Oh, hey, Dad. Did you happen to move the rock I put in the storage bin?" I ask.

"Noooo," he says. I can tell he's wondering what that missing rock has to do with our lying on the floor with our heads covered.

I raise my eyebrows at Ethan and Sadie. It's official. *Someone stole the code. Something dirty is going on in Zion.*

# - 13 -

I settle into the tent we had set up right behind the camper. "Ethan, who do you think stole the rock?"

He's got his sleeping bag hood pulled tight around his face. "Probably the man we saw studying it, who I think was Packman." The sleeping bag string pushes his cheeks forward, and it dangles near his chest. "Or it could have been Ranger Rob."

"What?" I sit up straight at the thought.

"How on earth could a park ranger afford a brand-new car like that one—for cash, no less? But the real question is, who left the garbage I paid so dearly to rescue, and what are they doing in the park?"

· Zion Gold Rush ·

"I wish I knew." I snap on my flashlight and complete two more Tara Tarantula pages. But after looking at the cartoon spider in my Junior Ranger booklets, I think about real ones. *They do live here, and they're huge.* That thought makes me start slapping my legs, imagining spiders everywhere. *Note to self: do not work on Junior Ranger booklets right before bedtime.*

Still, it's great to be in a tent. I rest quietly, looking at the moonlight filtering in. The silver light flickers, then complete darkness falls. *That's what happened to Sadie. The thick clouds have gotten stuck over her life.* Hating Jenna for what she'd done to my sister would be easy, but deep inside, I know it wouldn't be right. *I sure would like to help my sister through this hurt.*

Ethan clicks on a flashlight with a strange bluish light. When he holds up his palm, his skin is shining a brilliant neon-green.

"What on earth did you do to your hand?"

He grins. "It's black light powder we made in

school. I liked the green best. You can only see it when a black light shines on it. Pretty cool, huh?"

"I'll say!"

He clicks off the light. "Do you hear that?" Ethan asks, propping himself up on one elbow. He looks like a burrito in that sleeping bag.

"Yeah." I cock my head. "It's an engine. Probably a diesel."

"That's weird. No one's supposed to be driving around the canyon except the shuttles, and they quit at five."

I scurry out of my sleeping bag and unzip the tent. Far down the canyon road, the beams of headlights bounce off the canyon walls. I can just trace out its path as the engine revs, pulling up the incline.

"Something is definitely going on, and I'm thinking we're the only ones who know about it," Ethan declares when I share my report.

"What does it all add up to?"

"That is the million-dollar question, my friend."

## Zion Gold Rush

I sigh and chew on the strange code beginning 10N. *What on earth could that mean?* The tingle in my chest tells me the letters and the numbers are the key to everything.

The gentle patter of rain and then a searing flash of light wakes me fully, but the sharp crack of thunder bolts me upright. The thunder rolls over and over through the canyons. Ethan is sitting straight up too, and his wide-eyed expression without any noticeable eyebrows makes me laugh.

Another snap of light makes me cover my head.

I hear it sizzle, and then it sounds as if the thunder is tearing apart the air.

"Whoa! That was close," Ethan says, his cheeks still smooshed up by the sleeping bag.

A different rumble makes the rocks under the tent rattle. "What was *that*?"

# -14-

"Um. Thunder," Ethan says, as if it's obvious.

"No, it sounded different."

The next strike is farther away, and it lacks the sizzling crack that the closer one had. Still, on the tail end of the thunder is another distinct rumbling sound.

"You mean that?" Ethan asks.

"Yeah."

"Sounds like rocks or something. Maybe an avalanche," he says, but the thunder nearly drowns out his words. Rainwater drips into the tent, and I shift into a pool of cold water.

"Boys, come in now!" Mom's desperate cry has

me on my feet in a New York second. I pull open the tent zipper and literally breathe in rain. I sprint for the camper door where Mom and Dad gather me in.

"Where's Ethan!?" she shouts, over the howling of the storm.

"He was right behind me!"

The next strike is so close, it blinds me for a second. I turn, catching sight of Ethan hopping desperately, his sleeping bag tight around his face. His arms flail inside the fabric of the wet bag.

"Hurry!" I shout. The thunder makes him jump higher, but he goes down hard, trapped in the sleeping bag.

Dad and I rush out the door, and together we haul Ethan up, grabbing his elbows through the fabric. As we struggle forward through the crazed motion of the wind, the sky lights up, and everything is crystal clear for a heartbeat. In the distance, I see a flash of bright light coming from a canyon, but I nearly trip, so I focus ahead of us. As we run, I hear again the odd rumbling sound that shivers the ground.

Ethan trips on the stairs. Dad and I grip the bag and literally throw him in like a sack of flour. Dad slams the door behind us.

"Don't get close to the windows," Mom says.

Scared, Sadie rushes into Mom's arms. Ethan flops on the floor, and Dad has to get his pocket tool to untie the wet string around his face before we can unzip the sleeping bag.

Ethan finally emerges. "I'm wet…again."

Soaked to the skin, Ethan, Dad and I stand there dripping. A laugh tickles in my chest until I have to let it out, and soon we're all giggling.

"Let's get some towels, Sadie. I think the sleeping bag should go back outside in the rain. It's making a lake in here. I'll dry it out tomorrow."

We sleep late the next morning, and Mom looks up from her phone after breakfast. "The trails are closed due to the flooding after last night's storm. Two cars were swept away from the main parking lot."

## Zion Gold Rush

"Wow!" I say around a mouthful of cereal.

"Don't talk with your mouth full, Isaiah."

I catch Ethan sneaking a duplex cookie into his mouth between bites of cereal. I roll my eyes at him, but he just grins.

"Would you all rather stay here at the camper or head back to the Dino Museum?"

"Museum!" Sadie shouts.

"Yeah, me *too*," I say, wanting to see Dad's work.

"You might be a *two*, but I'm a *ten*, so me ten," Ethan says dramatically.

That comment makes Mom roll her eyes. We all smash our faces against the rental car window when Dad maneuvers along the higher end of the visitor center parking lot. Boulders and mud are piled high across the entire pavement.

"Can you imagine how much water it took to move that rock? It's nearly the size of this car!" Dad says, easing over a wash of gravel.

"I'm just glad we can get out! I need to get more groceries," Mom adds.

I shiver, remembering the incredible power of the storm, but the image of the sudden flash of bright light rising from the canyon floor makes me shake my head. I know lightning did not cause that fiery light. Avalanches caused by the storm could have caused the strange noises—but not the light.

We pull up to the Dinosaur Site long before I come to any conclusions.

---

Walking through the doors is like stepping back in time.

"Wow!" Seeing the prints the second time is just as amazing.

"Hey, Greg," Dixie says. "I bet your kids are eager to see your work."

"If you don't mind," Dad answers.

"Sure! Come on back, everyone."

We step through the Staff Only door, and I hear the familiar whir of the 3D printer as it lays down layer after layer of hot plastic film, building the dinosaur bone replicas a little at a time.

"It's a vertebra, right?" I ask, leaning in close. The machine is making an exact copy of every detail in plastic instead of bone.

"Yes, you're a smart one. Here are the other ones your dad has already finished."

She hands me a plastic version of a jaw fragment with two huge teeth still embedded in it.

"It's amazing!" I say, then hand it to Sadie.

"Yes, it will be even better when the Smithsonian classifies these."

Dixie hands me another plastic bone. "I have no idea what this one is." Dixie laughs. "And I have spent my entire life studying dinosaurs."

"Zion has plenty of those."

"Dinosaur bones?" she asks.

"Maybe. I meant *mysteries*."

"It is an incredible place, that's for sure," Dixie replies.

Ethan snaps his fingers, opening his backpack. "Excuse me, would you be able to tell us anything about this rock?"

He pulls out the small chunk that had broken off the slab with the code.

"Ethan!" Sadie hisses, "I thought that was with the big one!"

The three of us huddled around the fragment with 7S 3D scratched on it.

"I completely forgot I had it till just now! I was going to put it in the camper with the other one, but I grabbed the cookie first, and...well, that was that." He stuffs another in his mouth.

Sadie draws us closer, her voice low. "It's illegal to move rocks from a national park! Now we really have done something wrong." All the stress she's been dealing with is right there on her face.

"Sadie," I whisper. Needing her to hear me, I gently take her elbow. "You did nothing wrong—not now, and not...before."

"Isaiah's right. Besides I'll give it back to the rangers today," Ethan says lightly, completely unaware of how close Sadie is to losing control. She turns away, rushing to bury her face against Mom.

## Zion Gold Rush

Ethan turns back to Dixie. "Here you go."

"Well, for starters, it's limestone that has recently been carved from a larger rock."

Ethan and I exchange glances. *Dixie sure knows her rocks.*

"Can you tell us how old the markings are?" he asks.

"Let's take a peek with old Betsy."

"Excuse me?" Ethan says.

"Oh, sorry. That's my microscope. We spend so much time together, I thought she needed a name." Dixie slides into a chair and adjusts the scope, then she slides the rock fragment underneath.

She sighs as she squints through the microscope. "The weathering on the edges of the letters is minimal… Ah! There is still a fleck of metal embedded in the rock's grain from the tool that made it, I would assume."

She turns some more knobs. "The metal looks like a mixture of iron and nickel, which was used heavily at the end of the eighteenth century. I would say these numbers and letters were etched into the rock somewhere around 100 years ago. Here, take a look."

Ethan leans in to look. "Whoa! I can see everything you saw!"

Sadie comes over, wiping her eyes. I nudge her ahead.

"Oh, it's amazing!" she exclaims as she looks through the scope. It seems like an hour passes before she's done looking, and I bite my tongue hard to hold back a comment that would ruin my giving her the first turn.

Finally, my eye is against the soft rubber top of the microscope. *Dixie is right; the fleck of metal that we couldn't even see is pinched in the crevice of the letter D.*

"So, it's not an Indian petroglyph, which would have been very precious," she says. "This is what we like to call historic graffiti."

"Gra...what?" Sadie asks.

"Graffiti is an illegal marking or painting of

public property. Many times it makes something beautiful look ugly."

"Oh." This explanation seems to soothe Sadie's nerves. At least we hadn't lost an artifact. Ethan tucks the rock back into his pack, then stuffs two duplex cookies into his mouth. *He's making me hungry.*

I nudge him with my elbow. "How many of those do you have?"

He smiles while he chews. "Let's just say I packed two sets of clothes, some money, and plenty of *duplex cookies.*"

"Ohhh…."

"Your dad needs to scan one more item that cannot be touched. How would you like to look at an actual dinosaur egg?"

"Yeah!" we all shout.

# -15-

"I think we had better take a higher elevation trail today," Mom says the next morning.

"How did they get the parking lot cleaned up so fast?" I ask. The rocks and mud are gone; only a coating of dust now remains.

"I think that sort of thing happens here frequently, so they have plenty of practice. The shuttles are only running up to Stop 5 today. The water is still too high for the Narrows to be safe."

We walk to the nearly deserted visitor center and hand over the small chunk of code to Ranger Rob.

"No harm done, kids. Thanks for doing the

right thing though. It's great to see good families in Zion." I'm shocked to see his eyes mist up. "Makes me miss my grandfather. He passed not long ago and left everything he had to me."

Mom smiles at him sadly, and I elbow Ethan. "Well, that theory is a dud," I whisper.

He nods stroking his chin.

"We'll take the shuttle to Stop 5, Canyon Junction, and then we'll hike back to the visitor center," Mom says.

I stare hard at the driver; it's not Floyd today, and this driver doesn't make any strange comments to the passengers. My suspicions grow as I remember the revving engine winding up the canyon right before the storm. *But what was the shuttle doing—driving up here in the middle of the night?*

We get off the bus and find Mr. Carson adjusting his pack.

"Good morning!" Mom says with a wide smile.

"It's a good day for a hike!" he says. "Are you all taking the Pa'rus Trail?"

"Yes, sir," I answer.

"Suppose we could walk together for a spell?"

I nod, thinking *there's no way a man that old will keep up with us.* But he proves me wrong. In fact, the pace he sets soon has me dragging in heavy breaths.

"Come on, let's take a quick detour," Mr. Carson says a while later.

We look at Mom, who shrugs with a fake frown that says, "Why not?"

We cut down what looks like a deer trail and then duck under an amazing stone arch.

"Looky here," Mr. Carson says, pointing at the bright-red cliff.

We all suck in a breath. This section of cliff is sheltered from the sky by an overhang, and it's covered in odd-looking pictures of cows, people, and animal tracks.

"Are these real?" Ethan whispers in awe.

"Well, you're not dreaming, so I suppose they are," Mr. Carson says with a friendly laugh.

## Zion Gold Rush

"But, I mean…they're old—like from the Native American Indians?"

"Well, the Fremont Indians left most of the petroglyphs in Zion. They were an agricultural people, peaceful and strong. They left these messages to tell each other what seasons they should move the animals to new pastures and when to plant different crops."

If someone had told me that we were going to see some pictures drawn by Nataive American Indians who lived a thousand years ago, I wouldn't have been that excited. But standing here looking at them, the weight of all those years and time seems to rest in the air itself. I can't help but wonder if a Fremont Indian boy and I might have run races and played together.

"What's that sound?" Sadie asks.

Mr. Carson cocks his head. I squint, listening hard.

"It's an airplane," Ethan states, still studying the petroglyphs.

"Not that sound! Listen," Sadie says.

A few seconds later, I catch a faint rustling in the distance. "It could be the wind."

She shakes her head, "Mom, may I go and see?"

"Not by yourself. Boys?"

"I'll go," Ethan says, and I nod.

Sadie strides off, and we hurry to catch up. She takes my arm, coming to a sudden stop. "There! Surely you heard that!"

# -16-

"Um. No."

"Well, be quiet now. It's just ahead—whatever *it* is we're hearing."

That dinosaur feeling overtakes me, and my nerves intensify as goosebumps race across my arms. We creep around the cliff face, and Sadie goes still as stone, pointing silently ahead.

We see a thick green tangle of briars tucked against the rock, and this time I hear the sound clearly when the vines move. I also see a flash of brown hide, and for a second, I'm back at the Smoky Mountains with Cranky the Bear thundering toward me.

Sadie's grip on my arm tightens. "There are no bears in Zion, remember?" she whispers.

Funny that she knew exactly what I was thinking. "How do you know?" I murmur.

"I asked a ranger when we first got to Zion."

"Well, what is it then?" Ethan is on high alert, crouched low and ready to run. "A triceratops?"

Sadie kneels down and then gasps. "It's a bighorn ram, and he's caught in the briars!"

Now I can make out one of his front legs. It's at an odd angle—not quite resting on the ground.

"He needs help!" Sadie says.

*There will be no getting her away from here now.*

"Ethan," I say, "run for Mom and Mr. Carson."

He takes off faster than a deer, and Sadie and I carefully ease up to the briars. They shake hard, then go still, and I can hear uneven breaths coming from under the leaves.

"He could be hurt. Aw, he's trembling! Poor fellow. Come on, we've got to get him loose."

Sadie tries to push her way into the bushes, but

the sharp thorns soon draw dots of blood from her arm. "Ouch!"

"Watch out," I say, pulling Poppa's knife from my pocket. The stems are harder than I had figured they would be to cut through. Mom, Ethan, and Mr. Carson quickly arrive.

"Whoowee!" Mr. Carson exclaims. "I don't see a thing."

In response to his words, the bush goes wild, looking like a giant bobblehead. "Oh, my, I believe there is a ram in there. Let me see." Mr. Carson slowly eases down to one knee, muttering, "Once I get down here, I may as well stay a while. His horns are badly tangled in the briars. His eyes are glazed over, which means he's extremely dehydrated. Another couple of hours, and help wouldn't do him any good."

"What do we do?" Sadie asks, determined to help free the ram.

"Boys, cut a way in as quickly as you can. Girl, you find a pan or a dish. He needs water first thing and certainly before we let him loose. In his condition, he'll die before he reaches a stream."

Ethan and I work together, chopping at the sharp bush. The ram groans pitifully, and we double our efforts, ignoring the resulting scrapes and cuts from the briars.

Behind me, I can hear Sadie sawing a water bottle in half. The knife is loud as it rips through the plastic. Sweat pours down my back and evaporates quickly in the dry air. The rocks push the punishing heat of the sun onto us like an oven. Sadie wades into the bush, pulling the trail we've made open wider.

"Wait," she says, reaching through the leaves. "I'm touching him!"

"Okay, the thing we can't to do is cut him loose without a drink," Mr. Carson said. "Boys, come on back, and let the girl give him a drink."

"My name is Sadie."

"That's nice, girl. Don't waste a second."

Sadie takes the bottom half of the water bottle

and eases it down through the tangle. She puts it right up to his lips until they are dripping.

"He won't drink," Sadie says, near tears again.

"Thought as much," Mr. Carson says. "There's a point during dehydration that the taste of water seems hateful."

"Hang on!" Ethan digs through his pack. "I have some of those powder packets of Gatorade. Do you think that will help?"

The old man nods. "Sure would, boy."

We mix it in, and now the water is bright blue and smells like raspberry. I catch Sadie's worried glance. She shrugs. "I can't do anything right, remember?"

I put one hand on her shoulder. "Remember when you sang me across that log when we were in the Smokies? You saved my life back then! You never wondered if you could do anything good back then; you just did it."

She nods, still nervous.

"Trust now like you did then," I encourage.

She sighs and presses back into the bush. She dips her fingers into the blue water and tries to get a drop into the ram's mouth. The bush goes wild, and the ram's hooves scramble hard when her fingers touch his lips.

"Sadie!" Mom cries.

"It's okay, Mom. He's wound up so tight, he can't hurt me." Sadie takes a deep breath, her voice wavers at first, then grows into a sweet song.

"Sadie had a little ram, a little ram, a little ram, whose heart was made of gold…"

I watch the ram's weak struggling cease.

Sadie eases her dripping fingers up to the ram's lips again. He shudders at her touch, but he doesn't try to leap back from her.

"Ethan, that critter just has to drink for Sadie's sake. If he dies, I don't know what she'll do."

She dips her fingers again and eases them onto his dry tongue. This time he licks it up.

"Keep singing," I whisper, caught up in the ram's survival and the strange connection that I can almost feel forming between my sister and the bighorn.

"Everywhere that Sadie went, the ram was sure to go…" She sings sweet and high as the ram sighs, then reaches out to lick her wet fingers. Soon she eases the cutoff bottle through the tangle again. His nose twitches once, then he reaches for the liquid life and slurps it up.

Sadie's shoulders relax as he drains the bottle, searching for more. She turns with the biggest grin on her face I've ever seen.

*Oh, wow, the singing worked!*

"Boys, now cut that tight vine around his stomach first."

We step in and find it difficult to get our knives between the vine and his skin.

"Now, see there's one wrapped around his back leg. He'll be touchy about that one though. Don't let him kick you."

Ethan and I press into the briars, ignoring the many scrapes and cuts for the thorns. The bighorn goes wild when I touch his leg, but the vines still hold him in their grip.

"Isaiah!" Mom cries as I pull back.

"We're okay, Mom. He still can't move far, but he's just got to hold still," I grunt.

"Here, let me in," Sadie says confidently. She goes straight to the ram's head and slowly sets her palm against his wide brown forehead. As soon as she sings again, the ram's eyes no longer show their white rim of fear. Sadie nods, and Ethan takes hold of the vine.

"Ouch! Okay, Isaiah. I think it's safe to cut it now," he whispers.

# -17-

I saw vigorously at the woody vine, and it finally lets loose with a snap. The ram stands up on all four hooves for the first time in what might be days.

I move to release his horns—the last part of him that's bound. Sadie keeps her hand in place and a song on her lips. I'm shocked when I see that the vines have actually left marks on the hard bone of his heavy curved horns.

When only one more vine is left, I look at Sadie and hand her the knife. Then Ethan and I step back and kneel next to Mr. Carson.

I notice the ram's eyes aren't glazed over anymore. *I think he'll make it.*

"Be careful," Mom whispers, her hand over her heart.

Sadie nods, then forces the knife between the bone and the vine. As the vine lets loose with a pop, the ram's head sags. Then he shakes it weakly.

Sadie closes the knife and steps back slowly through the opening we'd made. The ram takes an unsteady step forward.

"Come on, boy," Sadie says softly. "You're free; you get to live."

He steps forward, following Sadie. When he's on open ground, he turns toward her. Time seems to slow down as he seems to dip his huge head in her direction.

"You're welcome," she whispers, as if she had heard him speak.

He steps off, and we watch each step become steadier. Right before he disappears around the bend, he turns back toward Sadie one more time. What passes between them is a secret only they know.

## Zion Gold Rush

We all sag with relief when he steps out of sight. Mom wraps Sadie in a relieved hug.

"Well, boys," Mr. Carson says, "I'm stuck. I may need a hand to get up."

Ethan and I reach out to take his arms, but he's even more unsteady than the ram. We have to hold him up for a while till he's solid.

"Might be a good time for some refreshment…" Mr. Carson says as we help him ease one hip onto a boulder.

"That's a great idea, Mr. Carson!" Mom says. The rest of us settle onto the hot sand. I didn't realize how much effort it had taken to free the ram.

Ethan, of course, pulls a duplex cookie from his pack.

Mom had packed some potato chips and cucumber slices. I save the cucumbers till last; they're my favorite. I hear the skittering sound of a small creature in the sand and turn to find a chipmunk staring at me. He puts his paws together in the air as if begging.

"Aw," Sadie says.

Just in time, Mom reminds, "Remember, we're not supposed to feed them."

I had readied a chip for him.

In minutes, we're surrounded. At least ten chipmunks are scampering all around us. Soon, they grow bolder, one sits on the toe of my boot, watching me. Sadie has been perfectly still with one hand extended. A chipmunk climbs into her palm.

"Whoa!" I say as another chipmunk emerges from under a rock. "That one is like a prehistoric-sized one." He's nearly twice the size of the others with a darker patch of fur on his head. For a moment he surveys the scene like an ancient king. Then his nose twitches, and he dives straight for Ethan's pack.

"Hey!" Ethan shouts. "You thief!" He rushes for his pack, no doubt filled with his precious duplex cookies. "Get out, *you...*" He reaches into his pack and fishes around. The huge chipmunk, with both cheeks stuffed full of cookies and one more

# Zion Gold Rush

that won't quite fit in his mouth, races straight up Ethan's arm.

When Ethan's howling frightens the chipmunk, the cookie thief disappears into his sleeve, and

Ethan goes wild, twisting and bucking, screaming long and loud.

"Help me!"

The chipmunk, with the third cookie still firmly in place, pokes his head out of Ethan's shirt collar. Ethan slaps frantically at his neck, and Mr. Carson nearly falls off his rock laughing. Sadie and I rush forward. Ethan writhes on the ground as if he's been electrocuted.

"Ethan," I shout, "be still!" My main concern is that he'll crush the chipmunk.

"There he is!" Sadie points at the wiggling lump under Ethan's shirt.

"AARRHHHH!" Ethan rolls hard to the left.

"Wait!" Sadie cries, and the chipmunk's head appears again in his sleeve opening.

I leap for him, but he's long gone by the time I smack Ethan's arm. I watch the little lump race down under Ethan's armpit and across his stomach. I can't tell if Ethan is crying or laughing.

Ethan squeals, and then the chipmunk shoots

out his pant leg and makes a beeline for a hole in the rocks.

"Oh, no, you don't!" Ethan's now on his feet, racing after the cookie thief.

"Ethan, stop! Didn't you learn your lesson at the Smokies? Remember the skunk?" Sadie shouts.

Ethan turns in midstride to yell, "This is war! He stole my cookies! He's…a Chiptomunkus Rex!"

Ethan dives for the ground, jamming his arm as deep as it will go into a hole.

*They can probably hear Mr. Carson laughing all the way back to the campground.*

"No!" Ethan shouts.

"It's hopeless; he's long gone," I say.

Ethan flattens himself out on the ground to get a better view. "No, he isn't! He dropped one; I can see it right there!"

"It's been in that rodent's mouth! Do you really want it back?" Sadie asks.

"It's MY cookie! Give it back, Chiptomunkus Rex, or so help me, I'll…I'll…"

"You'll what? Shrink yourself?"

My comment sends Mr. Carson into another fit of laughter.

"Isaiah, I'll prove it. There's a laser pointer in my pack. Go get it."

I find it in the bottom covered in cookie crumbs and join him in front of the crevice. He clicks on the power, and the red dot it produces lands solidly on the chocolate duplex cookie that's soggy on one end and has teeth marks in the middle.

Ethan sucks in a breath. *"There he is."*

I lay a little flatter on the ground and watch the critter sneak forward and snatch at the cookie. Ethan's fingers are nowhere near the chipmunk though he's reaching as far as he can.

"No!" Ethan's fists slam the ground, making the red dot bounce around in the crevice. The chipmunk has stuffed the last cookie into one cheek already, so he pounces on the light with both front paws.

"Aha!" Ethan whispers, carefully aiming the laser pointer. "I've got you now, Chiptomunkus Rex. Come to Papa."

The creature chases the red light closer and closer. Then a shadow races over our backs, and a chipmunk still out in the open gives a loud chirp. In a wild rush, they all sprint over our backs and heads and scamper down deep into the crevice.

We stare at the empty dark space. "You lost," I whisper.

Ethan's forehead hits the dirt, fake weeping. "Three cooookkkkiiieeessss!"

I stand up, slapping dust out of my clothes.

"A hawk scared them," Sadie says.

Ethan tucks the laser pointer into his back pocket and zips his backpack tight.

"You almost had them," I say, trying to console him.

He sighs, looking at the tiny scratches from Chiptomunkus Rex racing up his arm. "The worst part is, he used me as a means of escape! He's smarter than he looks."

I have to bite my lip to keep from laughing at him.

Mom and I help Mr. Carson stand up straight. He seems much better after the rest.

"Thank you very much. I'm not as good as I once was, but if I stay off my knees, I can still out-hike strapping young people like yourselves."

*I see a competitive glint in his eye.*

"Really?" Ethan says, ready for a battle he believes he can win.

"Aye."

"What do we get if we win?" Ethan asks.

"You would get the inner joy of having beaten me, but you won't."

Ethan, Sadie, and I smile at each other. *He's got to be like 85 years old.*

By the time we reach the visitor center, we're dragging in breaths, neck and neck with Mr. Carson, except he's hardly puffing.

He reaches out and touches the building first. "Beat you."

## Zion Gold Rush

I lean against the wall, and the rumble of the shuttle's engine makes me turn.

"Look," I pant, nudging the others. "Floyd is at the wheel, and his fenders are full of dirt."

# - 18 -

"I don't see any," Sadie says.

"Not on the paint—up around the wheel wells. None of the other shuttles have anything like that. That's because they only stay on the pavement."

"You're right," Ethan mutters, crossing his arms.

"He could've gotten it during the mudslide the other day," Sadie says logically.

I frown. *Her explanation is a possibility.* We watch the passengers disembark, then Sadie gasps, gripping my elbow. Packman walks easily down the aisle, and then he leans over to Floyd, passing him a slip of paper. Floyd shifts his eyes from side to side, trying not to look suspicious, then tucks the paper into his pocket. Packman steps off the bus. He pulls at the shoulder strap, and his pack shifts easily on his back. *It's empty.*

Ethan's eyes narrow. "Wait a minute, what hiker heads out with a full pack and returns with an empty? "

"Okay, guys," Sadie says. "He's the same one who was looking at the historical graffiti that Ethan cracked off. I think we have something here."

That feeling tingles in my chest—the one that's been so faithful to warn me of danger.

"What did he pass to Floyd?" Ethan asks.

I snap my fingers, "Floyd is the one who drove up the canyon the other night! I'll bet he's been using the shuttle after hours, moving dinosaur bones. Why else would the shuttle be so dirty?"

"Hang on!" Ethan takes off his pack and digs through it. "I have an idea." He grabs a small bottle and rushes toward Floyd's shuttle. The crowds are still thin since the Narrows aren't open yet, and he leaps up onto the first wide step, then trips on the second one and sprawls forward toward Floyd. The cap comes off the bottle in his hand and powder explodes forward. A cloud of it floats between Floyd and Ethan.

"Ethan, come off there!" Mom shouts, catching up.

"Oh, sure, Aunt Ruth." He skips down the steps, waving sheepishly at Floyd and comes over with a wide grin. "Perfect."

"What did you do?" Sadie asks, inspecting the small bottle in his hand.

"I set a trap. Now we can track him."

"Your black-light powder?" I ask.

"Precisely, my dear Watson."

"Now," Ethan clicks on his flashlight with the strange bluish beam. "We can see where he goes." Ethan's clothes light up with an odd, bright-green color.

"Sadie," Mom calls, "let's head to the bathroom before we walk back to camp. Boys, stay in sight of the building."

## Zion Gold Rush

"Sure, Mom," I say, my thoughts running wild. Floyd pulls his shuttle around to the back of the visitor center, and I check my watch. It's five o'clock. "How about another trap?"

"What do you have in mind?" Ethan asks.

"We tie a string from the parked shuttle to the fence. If it's broken before the first run tomorrow, we know Floyd has been using it after dark."

Ethan smiles. "Not bad, Rawlings, not bad!"

# -19-

Early the next morning I creep up to the room where Mom and Dad are sleeping.

I must admit, being in the RV has been sort of fun—not like tent fun—but escaping a thunderstorm when you need to surely is nice.

It's so early that Dad hasn't left for the dinosaur museum yet. I know he'll say yes, and he's only half awake, so I nudge his arm. "Dad, can we run down to the visitor center and then come right back?"

"What time is it?" he mumbles.

I click on the soft green light of my watch. "5:25 a.m. It's sunrise."

He waves one hand. "Don't be gone too long."

## Zion Gold Rush

"Thanks, Dad." I slip out of the room, hoping not to wake up Mom. Ethan and Sadie are waiting anxiously.

"He said yes," I whisper.

We fake high-fives to avoid the sound and then step carefully down the loud RV steps, trying not to rock the camper and wake up Mom.

Running down the path with the golden light glinting off the cliffs feels like racing into heaven. A million spiderwebs are white with dew glistening in the early morning sun, and songbirds swoop through the fog.

We slow to a walk at the empty visitor center. I hold my breath as we approach Floyd's bus.

"It's broken!" Sadie says, pointing at the string hanging from the back of his bus.

"I knew he was up to something," I add.

Ethan clicks on his black light, and the area outside the folding door of the shuttle lights up bright green. Floyd's footprints are everywhere.

"Seems like he should've just gotten off the bus

once when his shift ended, doesn't it?" Ethan says, pointing the light toward the rear of the bus.

There's practically a runway of boot prints that disappear around the back of the bus.

"Let's follow them."

Sadie looks back toward the Watchman Campground, biting her lip.

"Absolutely." Ethan steps onto the sand where the prints are far less crisp around the back of the bus.

"There are no bears in Zion," Sadie says to herself. We follow the trail past a pure white boulder.

"Look!" The prints end at a large flat square impression on the ground.

"They carried something from here to the bus, and whatever that item was, it was heavy. Then they drove it up to the canyon last night," I say.

"So, what do we do about it?"

"First, we check on our garbage evidence; it should be right over there. It's funny how close these two stashes must've been, yet we didn't see this one. Next, we convince Mom to take us back to where we found the code. I'm sure it's a map of some sort."

"A map? It's just a jumble of letters and numbers."

I shake my head. "No, it was important enough for them to steal; it has to lead to what they are trying to hide."

I'm relieved when we find the garbage still well covered. By the time we're back at the camper, we've covered every possible idea of what they could be doing—from alien invasions to the last living dinosaur on earth.

Dad steps out of the camper just as we arrive.

"Good morning! I'm setting up my last print today of the dinosaur egg. I might just get done early. Maybe we can go hiking together."

"Yeah!" I hug him tight and fight off the twinge I always feel when he leaves for work.

Sadie turns to me with a smile after he pulls out. "Maybe they found the largest pirate treasure ever."

I shake my head, looking fondly at her. I sure am glad she had found that ram. Saving him had seemingly made her remember who she really is. "We're like hundreds of miles from any ocean."

"You never know." She turns to Mom; her eyes go wide, but she keeps her mouth shut.

"I know I'm sunburnt. I must look like a lobster," Mom says.

"Does it hurt?" Sadie asks.

Mom nods. "But I don't want you all to be stuck here with me in the shade all day. I called Mr. Carson, and he said he would take you through the park for today if you like."

"That would be great!" *This is just what we need!*

Mom turns to call him back, catching the door with her shoulder, "Ouch."

A few minutes later, we're heading back to the visitor center to meet Mr. Carson.

"Do you think we can get him to go back to the West Bank Trail?" Sadie asks.

"With my good looks?" Ethan says, "Sure!"

"Or maybe you could offer to go to war with another chipmunk. I bet he hadn't laughed that hard in years," I say.

"True," Ethan admits.

"Are those the same jeans you were wearing yesterday?" Sadie asks.

"Yup. And they're the same ones I'll wear tomorrow. I only brought two pairs, and the other ones would never let go of the dumpster smell, so I threw them out."

"I do appreciate you doing that," Sadie says.

# -20-

"Kids," Mr. Carson waves a knobby arm. But I won't let him fool me this time; the old man is strong as long as he has both feet on the ground.

"Hi!" Sadie greets him.

"Where shall we head today, troops?"

"The West Bank Trail!" Ethan says.

"Well, you've got your minds made up; it sounds good to me."

"That was easy," Ethan says quietly, then adds louder, "Floyd isn't driving today?"

Mr. Carson crosses his arms in disgust. "Floyd McAllister called in sick today—just the same as his father used to do."

## Zion Gold Rush

"Or he's up to his eyeballs in illegal activity," Ethan says barely under his breath.

"What's that?" Mr. Carson cups his ear.

"Nothing, sir."

It seems like only moments pass before we're at the spot on the trail where we need to turn off to reach the original code location.

I nudge Sadie. She bites her lip and shakes her head at me. I nod at her. "You ask," I whisper.

Finally, she rolls her eyes and clears her throat. "Um, Mr. Carson, what is that canyon over there called?" She points to the canyon where Packman had disappeared.

"Don't know that it has an official name, but I've always called it Little Angel. You know the rugged hike up to Angels Landing? I don't suppose you young'uns have done it. Anyway, this canyon splits into four forks and can get mighty confusing in there. But if you can find the right fork, it's got a view that'll take your breath away."

"Could we see?" Sadie asks.

"I suppose…if you have a mind to."

"We do," Ethan adds, following Mr. Carson off the trail with a smile.

"By the looks of it, plenty of folks been coming this way lately," Mr. Carson says, studying the ground as he crosses the small stream.

Ethan clicks on his black light, revealing barely a hint of brilliant green on the trail side of the creek, then nothing on the other. Floyd had definitely been through here—probably more than once. But the creek had washed the powder off his boots.

That feeling streaks across my chest, and I keep a sharper eye out as we walk.

"Now, you'll find this interesting…or not." Mr. Carson stops at the place where the code used to be.

"Well, I'll be. A fine piece of historical graffiti has been here since I laid eyes on this rock when I was just knee-high to a grasshopper."

"So…um…yeah…" Ethan chews on his lip. "I might have dislodged it earlier."

Mr. Carson turns to him. "Where is it now?"

## Zion Gold Rush

"It was stolen, sir." Ethan digs the toe of his shoe into the hot sand.

"Who would do such a thing?" Mr. Carson asks.

"We're sorry!" Sadie says.

*I can see all my sister's self-doubt crashing down hard again. Maybe this is a bad idea.*

"We were going to give it to a ranger, but it was stolen before we got the chance!" Her voice cracks on the last word.

"Easy now, girl. No harm done. I just wondered is all. Someone stole it, you say?"

I nod, and without intending to, I say, "We'd already found some suspicious garbage, and it seemed like the code might be part of its story."

"Suspicious garbage? Never heard of such a thing. What was it?"

Ethan gives me the stink eye for telling Mr. Carson, but he started it.

I tell Mr. Carson the first part of our garbage adventure—finding it discarded and cleaning up—but leave out the stinky half.

*"You say the boxes say Dyno Nobel?* Why that is the sole manufacturer of dynamite in the US of A."

Ethan says, "Dynamite?" Then he slaps the hand over his mouth, his surprised looking non-eyebrows even funnier.

*Dynamite.* Inside my head, I am back in the pouring rain, trying to get the "Ethan burrito" into the camper and seeing the strange cloud visible in the lightning bolt.

"What is it, boy? You've gone as white as a sheet."

"I… I…Someone was blasting two nights ago! They were using the storm to cover the explosions!"

"Who covered what explosions?" Mr. Carson's voice is growing higher in pitch at every turn.

"Floyd McAllister! We don't know what he's up to, but we tracked him with black-light powder right to the creek. Plus, he's been driving the shuttle after hours. His buddy Packman was the one we found first studying the graffiti," Sadie's eyes are wide too as the words pour out, then she slaps the hand over her mouth, realizing she's given away everything.

"Hold on now. Back up, kids, and tell me this whole story from the beginning."

We tell it all, including the strange interaction between Floyd and the man we call Packman. When we're done, Mr. Carson strokes his white stubbled chin, his eyes darting back and forth as he thinks. We hold our breath, waiting.

"Floyd McAllister. He always was a rotten egg." He looks down the canyon, I can nearly see the thoughts racing through his mind. "Blasting. Only one reason for that."

We lean in to hear, but he's quiet for so long I think he might never speak again.

# - 21 -

"What is the *one reason*?" I whisper, trying to be one with his consciousness.

"What's that? Oh, you ever heard the legend of the White Cliffs Lost Gold Mine?"

We turn slowly to look down the canyon. The walls here are *white* compared to the rest of Zion's red-and-yellow rock.

"You think?" Ethan's voice is quiet with awe.

"Sure wish we had that historical graffiti," Mr. Carson says.

"We do!" Sadie pulls her tracing from her pack.

"Ah, you're well-prepared, girl." Mr. Carson rubs his chin again. "N, S and F, B," he mutters.

"It's Sadie," she says, but Mr. Carson is busy studying her tracing.

"N and S are easy; that's north and south. Ten paces north. But what on earth could B and F stand for?" Mr. Carson mutters.

"Backward and forward!" Ethan says, nodding to himself confidently.

Mr. Carson's sharp gaze finds him. "Well, boy, you might just be right."

"It's Ethan," my cousin says.

Mr. Carson shrugs. "Any of you young'uns up for a hike through Little Angel—just a few paces at a time?"

"Yes, sir!" we say together.

"Ten paces north," Ethan says, stretching his long, beanpole legs into exaggerated steps. "Nine... ten. What's next?"

Ethan is staring straight up a cliff face about three inches from his nose.

"It just so happens that you should go 25 paces forward."

"Um…" Ethan stretches high with his equally beanpole like arms. "I don't think this is possible."

"It might help if you had started out heading *north*," Mr. Carson says flatly.

A curious shade of red creeps up Ethan's neck.

"Here," I say, pulling out my compass.

"Good job, boy! I would just go by the sun normally, but the compass will be far better." We head back to the smooth spot Ethan had created days ago.

"Let's see…" I hold the compass flat so the needle can swing freely. Sadie leans over it with me.

"North is that way." I point down the canyon, nearly the opposite direction that Ethan had paced. He repeats his high-kneed walk that reminds me of Tara Tarantula.

"Aha!" he says. This time the cliff is angled ahead of him, allowing us to move forward but not north any farther.

"Twenty-five! Feed me some more directions," Ethan says.

"Five back," I say, reading over Mr. Carson's shoulder.

"Why would we go back if we just went forward? Maybe it isn't back and forth at all." Ethan frowns.

"Let's just give it a whirl. These canyons can be mighty secretive." Mr. Carson is the first one to turn around and take five steps. "And there it is…"

## -22-

I gasp when I catch up and see the crack in the cliff wall that I would have missed entirely going the other direction.

Mr. Carson grunts as he squeezes into the tight opening. "You all stay there and go for help if this canyon proves too tight."

He takes another step and completely disappears. Even staring right at the crack, it's hard to believe that an opening is really there. The stone blends together perfectly. I put my hand into the crevice, trying to control the strong sensation in my chest.

"Guys! He's got the code. What if he has left us

here to get all the gold for himself?" Ethan's voice cracks in the middle of his sentence.

"First of all, any gold in Zion belongs to the national park. Second, what do you take him for? A pirate with a hook for a hand?" Sadie frowns at Ethan.

"ARRGGG!" A very piratic cry echoes from the crevice.

Ethan raises his brows. "See?"

"Girl! Come along, you've got another ram to rescue," Mr. Carson's voice is muffled.

Sadie darts past me, and I follow her into the crevice. A few steps later, her shoulders slump.

"You're no ram, Mr. Carson. But *you* do seem to be stuck."

Together, we work Mr. Carson's pack free from the overhang where it was snagged.

"Thank you," he says.

Ethan has his black-light on, shining it past our legs. Just ahead, on the pinched part of the walls, I see a wide spot of neon green.

"Floyd didn't wear the powder off his pants, did he? We are hot on their trail!" Ethan says.

"Check your compass, boy," Mr. Carson says strapping his pack on tighter.

I level it again, and sure enough, we're headed directly north. We follow the rest of the code, excitement growing as we near the end. But the last set of actions leads us to...*nothing!*

*Nothing at all.*

Sadie's arms flop at her sides. "I guess it was all a wild goose chase."

"No, we're just not done yet," Ethan says. "Remember the smaller chunk that broke off?"

"Of course!" she smacks her forehead. "We gave it to Ranger Rob. But I think it said 10S on it."

"No." Ethan squints, trying to remember. "It was 9F."

"You're both wrong; it was 12D," I assert.

"D? That doesn't even make sense." Ethan begins his tarantula walk, but he only gets six paces forward when he reaches a sheer cliff face.

"Which way is south?" Sadie asks, pursuing her own idea.

"That way." I point.

Seconds later, she is standing directly in the middle of the canyon. "I can't do anything right! How can I forget what was on that rock?"

"Well, where is the tracing of it?" Mr. Carson asked.

"There isn't one. It was somewhere else when I made the first tracing."

"D." I pluck at my lower lip, turning slowly in the hot valley. A steep slope right beside me runs into another smaller canyon. A little stream trickles out the bottom.

"D is for down," I say. Everyone else is busy searching the canyon walls for the distinct V-shape Hubble had described in the legend. Ethan is running his light carefully over the canyon walls.

Soon, I'm on step seven down. I drop down a little farther around a bend and follow the small stream. "Eleven…twelve," I count off my steps. "So, maybe it was 14?" I say to myself, then my mouth hangs open as I look up a massive V-shaped crack in the cliffs straight ahead. Sharply broken boulders are strewn around a dark opening.

I draw a breath to shout, but something rough, dark, and smelly covers my head.

## -23-

"Hey!" I shout, but strong arms crush the air from my lungs.

I struggle like mad, but the man grips me tighter. I feel the shock of cold water on my leg, then he forces my head nearly to my knees, and I trip forward through the slippery stream. Suddenly, everything is eerily quiet, as if he'd transported me to another planet. *Maybe the alien theory is correct.*

The air on my arms is cool, damp, and so still that I get goosebumps.

"What have you drug in?" a rough voice asks.

"Found him digging around at the entrance."

"Take off the bag," the first voice orders.

In one rough motion, the stiff fabric scrapes my face, catching on my nose.

"Ouch!" I say, and the anger that flares up is better than the fear. *We're in a cave by a small stream trickling into the rest of the world.*

Packman stares at me. I look over my shoulder. Of course, it's Floyd's iron grip that's making my upper arms shout in pain.

"What are you doing down here, kid?" Packman demands.

"He's after the gold, Will."

"Floyd! Will you ever learn to keep your mouth shut? Now they know my name!"

Floyd clamps his thick lips together with a frown.

"We can't very well let him go now." The man mutters something else under his breath. Then he slaps his leg in anger, which makes me jump. He's getting angry now as the reality of his plan being discovered settles in.

*I've ruined all his plans.*

## Zion Gold Rush

"Floyd," he says the name like an insult, "you should have just scared him off. You blew it!" Packman's face is growing a deeper shade of red, and I can't help leaning away from him in fear.

"Sorry, boss." He was looking at the entrance.

Packman flinches, then turns to me. "How old are you, kid?"

My mouth is too dry to speak, but when Packman growls and takes a menacing step toward me, I squeak out, "Twelve!"

The man's hands grip his hair. "No 12-year-old tourist kid is wandering this deep in the canyons alone, Floyd." He focuses hard on me. "How many people are with you?" He leans in, and his breath turns my stomach.

"I…" *I won't tell him about Sadie and Ethan; that would put them in danger.* "There's…an old man."

The man slaps his leg again, "Quick, tie him up on the ledge!"

Floyd's fingers feel like steel clamps as he forces me deeper into the cave.

Half my brain is searching for any weakness that would allow me to escape. The other half is cataloguing everything I see in the cave. The main opening is high and wide, but that quickly ends in a sheer back wall. *But wait—not a wall!* It's a high ledge—nearly 40 feet tall. They have rigged a pulley system bolted to the ceiling of the cave, and Floyd pulls me into an aluminum cage. He and I barely fit together on the small platform.

I twist, watching as Packman stomps on a pedal near the ground.

I hear a click, then a rope next to him moves. He grabs it and pulls.

I flinch as the three-sided cage starts to rise. "Quit it, kid!" Floyd growls in my ear, and I go still. *It's an elevator. But where does it lead?*

When we reach the top of the ledge, I feel dizzy. I've never been so thankful for someone pushing me as I am when Floyd shoves me onto the solid, smooth rock floor.

I look up and gasp. Ahead, glimmering in the

near darkness, are giant white crystals with their crisp points and symmetrical sides.

"Quit looking!" Floyd yanks me hard, and I grimace as he pulls a coil of rope off a large pile of supplies and binds my hands behind my back.

He ties me to an eyebolt anchor in the floor. I'm nearly centered in the wide space with my back toward the crystals.

# -24-

Floyd tosses the extra rope onto the supplies, then hurries back to the cage. Floyd tugs the rope, and in a few hand-over-hand motions, he disappears from my view.

When I yank hard at my rope, it bites into my skin. *I'm getting nowhere.* The darkness in the cave is deeper now without Floyd's headlight. The only place I can really see is near the ledge where a little sunshine from the outside seeps in from the distant, tiny entrance.

I swallow hard and hold my breath as a sound reaches me. It sure seemed like one of Sadie's shrieks when I catch her during hide and seek.

## Zion Gold Rush

"You'd better not hurt her!" I growl, yanking so hard against the rope I feel the strain in my neck.

"Or you'll what?" I ask myself. The truth settles hard in my stomach. My situation couldn't be much worse. *Two gold-hungry men with the biggest treasure trove in history to protect have me tied up in a cave.*

I freeze at the sound of shoes scraping the rocks.

"EEEHHH!" Ethan's voice is nearly a war cry as it echoes up onto the ledge. I strain to hear more. I hear a scuffle, then a grunt.

"Don't try that again!" Packman's warning sends shivers up my arms.

A metallic click echoes crisply in the dark. It's the sound of the foot pedal that releases the cage at the bottom. The rope moves through the pulley in the ceiling.

Floyd and Sadie soon appear. She has tears in her eyes as he forces her onto the ledge.

"Let her go!" I struggle wildly with zero results.

"Be quiet, kid."

Sadie's face is as white as a sheet.

*We've got to get out of here!*

Soon, Floyd has made another trip in the cage, and Sadie, Ethan, and I are tied back-to-back to the bolt. I take Sadie's thin, cold hands in mine. *The rope is too tight; it's cutting off her circulation.*

"Well. We're together again—*in a gold mine*," Ethan says, facing the crystals.

"Could have been under better circumstances," I grunt, searching for a way to loosen the ropes.

"True," he says, "but look at the streaks of gold in those crystals."

"No, thanks. I'm too busy trying to figure out how to get out of here," I grunt again.

"Whoa, now," Ethan says. "What we need to do is figure out how to get rid of Floyd and Packman. Imagine how much gold is in here."

"Ethan!" Sadie's voice is sharp. "Everything here belongs to the national park."

"Maybe we could get a finder's fee…or a percentage?"

## Zion Gold Rush

"Shhhh," I hiss.

More footsteps are echoing below. We freeze, listening hard.

"Floyd McAllister, I know your mother is rolling over in her grave at your behavior," Mr. Carson growls.

"You leave Mama out of this!" Floyd's voice wavers as he shouts at Mr. Carson.

"Just one more word, old man, and I'll make sure you'll never say another," Packman's icy voice threatens.

The familiar click makes me flinch, and soon Mr. Carson is also tied behind me, our shoulders jammed together.

"Clear anything off the ledge they could use to escape," Packman orders Floyd, then he clicks on the flashlight strapped to his forehead.

Ethan gasps, and I crane my neck to see. The crystals are thicker than my leg, and they glitter in the beam of light as far as I can see! As Packman heads deeper into the cave, the light reflects from the ceiling like a million prisms, sending tiny rainbows everywhere.

"So. Much. Gold," Ethan breathes.

"So it's true after all… Ouch!" Mr. Carson's voice is filled with pain.

"Are you all right, Mr. Carson?" I ask.

"It took the both of them to bring me down, but, oh, I feel a fire in my hip from the fall I took; that's for sure."

"Quiet!" Floyd orders as he loads ropes, canvas bags and other smaller items into the cage. Soon he's dropping down to the entrance, and we're alone again.

"How do we get out of here?" I ask in a low voice.

"And how much gold can we each carry?" Ethan adds.

I roll my eyes and then add, "What do they plan to do with us?"

"I don't think they even know yet," Mr. Carson says. "But think about it. Two men discover one of the largest gold veins in the U.S.—except they can't claim or buy it because it belongs to the national park. So, they're just going to steal it—one load at a time—nice and quiet. Now, we're here, and our presence has blown up their whole plan in smoke. I'd wager we need to make a hasty departure. Greed and desperation make bad bedfellows."

His words sink in, layer by layer, until the knot in my stomach feels like a brick.

The ceiling suddenly ignites with the million rainbows again. *Packman is returning.* He strides by us again, carrying a heavy black sack over one shoulder.

"So. Much. Gold," Ethan whispers again.

*Clearly, he's got gold fever.*

"Floyd!" Packman barks. "Never leave the cage down when I'm up here! How many times do I have to say it?"

"Sorry, boss, I was going to put it back up. I'm coming." Floyd's voice barely reaches us from the lower level. *Click.* The rope winds, and the cage arrives empty. A counterweight or something similar makes it possible for the lift to move easily.

We sit in silence for a moment after Packman lowers himself. Then Sadie and I erupt with desperate yanks and struggles. Mr. Carson sits still as stone against my shoulder. His calmness seeps into me. I realize I am not getting anywhere by struggling. Now my wrists are raw, and I think I've pulled a muscle in my arm.

"It should only take a few minutes for us each to gather a sack full," Ethan babbles.

"Mom and Dad will find us, right?" Sadie's voice is tight.

"Now listen up!" Mr. Carson's deep voice makes us go still. "What we need to do is to get everybody thinking clearly. Our main goal is getting out of here, right?"

"Right now!" Sadie responds.

"Yes, sir," I say. Facing away from each other as we talk feels weird. My eyes have adjusted to the dark, and I can make out the stack of familiar

## Zion Gold Rush

Dyno Nobel explosives. Beyond that, I can even make out the first row of gems.

"Right, Ethan?"

I have to give it to Mr. Carson; he knows what Ethan is planning.

"Um. Well. There is a bag over there. Wouldn't it be dumb not to bring out some evidence?"

"You can't keep even an ounce of this gold, boy. It's a part of Zion."

"What happened to that saying, *finders keepers*?" Ethan asks.

"We couldn't even keep a plain old rock, remember?" I say.

"But…but…but this is different. This is important," he sputters.

"You've got gold on your mind—same as Floyd and William," Mr. Carson accuses.

"I do not," he denies.

A sick silence descends on us for a second, and then he proves himself wrong.

"Nobody would miss it, see? It's just hanging

there on those crystals—not doing anybody a stitch of good."

Mr. Carson clears his throat. "Boy, if no one gave it to you, and you didn't buy it, then it isn't yours! If you take any of that gold, you'll be a thief—plain and simple."

"I'm not a thief!"

I can almost hear the wrestling match Ethan is having inside.

"Good. So, our main objective is getting out of here, right?"

I can hear our breathing in the damp air as the seconds roll by.

Ethan gives a long sigh. "You're right. But how do we do it? My hands are asleep they're tied so tight."

"Shhh," Sadie whispers.

At her warning, I cock my head. *Floyd and Will are returning.*

The two men ignore us entirely as they ride up in the cage and disappear into the crystal cave. It doesn't take them long to return with their sacks full. I catch snatches of their conversation as they near us again. "Leave them here."

"Folks would come searching."

"This mess is your fault, Floyd. You ought to be the one to clean it up. You're the one who ruined everything."

# -25-

*What does he mean—clean it up?* My blood runs cold.

They grow silent as they pass, and Sadie shrinks closer to me.

"All right, so how do we get out of here?" Ethan asks when they're gone.

"They keep the elevator locked at the bottom when they leave. Floyd took all the ropes. So, even if we got untied, we would still be trapped up here."

*Mr. Carson is right.*

"Aren't you supposed to be helping us feel calm?" Ethan yanks on his ropes again.

"Now, boy. Those are just the facts we must face.

## Zion Gold Rush

There's no point in running around with our eyes shut. Let's think for a bit." Minutes pass like slugs as the weight of our situation presses down.

*No one knows exactly where we are—especially not after we turned off the trail. Floyd and Will have every reason to make sure we never see the light of day again.*

Sadie releases my hands and begins to work at the knots.

"It's no use. We can't get loose." Ethan slumps behind me.

"He took my knife too," I add, longing for its sharp blade and the comfort of its long service to my family.

"You know, my great-great-grandpappy was the first man to paint Zion. The funny thing was, nobody believed it was a real place—not until they saw it with their own eyes. He had to convince them all. That story has a lesson for every sticky situation. We have choices to make every day. The question is whether or not we'll make the right one."

Sadie goes still.

*Mr. Carson's words have struck deep.*

"Right now, we need a miracle, so let's all agree to work together and find a way out of here."

Sadie's fingers start searching up and down the ropes again, her movements are smoother this time. She grunts, and I'm about to ask her what she found, but she beats me to words.

"What has a thumb and four fingers but isn't alive?" she asks as she shifts, smashing her shoulder into mine.

Ethan squeaks. "This is no time for jokes!"

"A glove." The words come out funny as she contorts herself even farther.

"What has a neck but no head?"

"Sadie," I groan. She's pushing on me so hard that the ropes are biting into my already sore wrists. "What are you…" Now she's practically on top of me.

"Ouch!" I shout as she steps on my hands. *Wait, how is she stepping on my hands?*

"My elbow doesn't bend that way!" I hear pain in Ethan's voice.

Sadie grunts again, nearly flattening us. "It does now." Then she answers her own joke: "A bottle." Her voice floats somewhere above me now.

"Who was tied up, but now is free?" she asks.

"Huh?" I say.

"I am!" she says lightly, stepping out of our circle, pulling the ropes from her hands.

"Nice move, girl," Mr. Carson says.

"How on earth did you do that, Sadie?" I stare up at her in awe.

"Mr. Carson is right. Listening to the wrong voice stinks. I've decided to listen and choose the right one. Listen!" She cocks her head.

"Sit down, girl! Hurry!" Mr. Carson whispers.

Sadie plunks next to me, and I take her now-warm hands in mine. We're all breathing hard from the excitement, and I hope the men won't notice. Will casts an angry stare toward us, and I hold my breath.

"The cage is up!" I whisper when they disappear into the mine.

"Should I run for help?" Sadie asks.

"Don't be too hasty now," Mr. Carson says. "That would leave three of us here tied up and trapped with two angry men. The girl has made good progress; let's bide our time for a bit more."

"It's Sadie," she says flatly.

The men pass by again, and we all lean hard together to cover the incriminating loose ropes. The elevator clicks at the bottom, and the men's shuffling footsteps echo away. I scowl. The noise seems to carry on for too long.

"Are they coming back?" I breathe out the words.

"No, they're gone," Sadie whispers. "That's something different…" she gasps, and we all crane our necks.

## -26-

"Chiptomunkus Rex!" Ethan growls. "Have you come to gloat? No way will you get my last cookie, you thief!"

"Shh. Nobody move!" Sadie says.

"Um. Yeah, we're tied up, remember?"

She ignores my comment. "Ethan, those are the same jeans you wore yesterday, right?"

"Yeah."

"Do you still have your laser pointer?" Sadie whispers, her eyes locked on the chipmunk's careful approach.

"Yeah, it's been poking me in the rear this whole time I've been tied up."

"I need it right now."

Ethan shifts, grumbling and pulling my ropes tighter. "Here, it's sticking out of my back pocket."

Sadie grabs it, "All right, Rex, you love to chase red dots, remember?"

She clicks on the laser, and the chipmunk crouches, his eyes locked on the target. He pounces with his little paws spread wide. She shuts it off just before he lands.

"That's right, Rex." She clicks it on again, closer to the ledge.

"Sadie, I don't think playing with my archnemesis is a great plan right now."

"Just let her work," I hush Ethan as Rex pounces again. I suck in a breath when she points the red dot at the rope dangling near the cliff's edge.

"You are brilliant, Sadie," I whisper.

She doesn't respond, but when Chiptomunkus Rex manages the long leap onto the ropes, she scurries forward to the ledge, carefully pointing the light farther down.

"Oh, please, it has to work."

"Make what work?" Ethan twists, unable to see. "What is going on?"

"Be quiet and listen for it," I say, shutting my eyes so I can hear better.

Heartbeats pass like hours. Sadie shifts the light again. *Click.* I flop back in relief against Ethan and Mr. Carson. "Yes!"

"Yes, what?" Ethan barks, then the cage rises.

"Fine job, girl! Ha-ha!" Mr. Carson crows a laugh, and Sadie guides the cage to a stop at the top with a huge smile. She takes a bow. "All aboard."

"But," I jerk at the ropes.

"Oh, right. You're still tied up." She rushes over, working frantically at our bonds.

"Rex jumped right on the release plate when I put the laser on it. I was worried he wouldn't be heavy enough to work the lever."

"You can thank me later. He was probably extra fat from the cookies he stole from me," Ethan grumbles.

I stand, stretching out the kinks. Mr. Carson needs help from all three of us to get on his feet. He grimaces, limping badly. Sadie and I help him into the cage, and a second later, Ethan jumps in.

"Going down," he says as he works at the ropes.

"There's not much time," Mr. Carson can't cover the pain in his voice as he clutches his hip. "We've got to get out quick. Leave me behind if you must. I'll only slow you down."

"No," Sadie and I say together as we step out of the cage at the bottom.

"Hurry," I say as we shuffle toward the low entrance. The two thieves have placed boards over the small stream. Our feet seem too loud on the wooden planks as we duck through the low entrance. The hot sun kisses my face, and I want to shout for joy. I would if danger wasn't so near. Then Sadie shrieks.

I whirl but Will already has one arm around her neck and the other clamped over her chest.

"Nobody move!" he snarls.

Mr. Carson had nearly fallen when Packman had snatched Sadie away from helping to support him, and now his weight pulls me slowly to one knee.

Ethan is a still as stone, just one finger twitches as he stares at the scene.

"You all get back inside the cave! Ain't no way I'll lose all this gold to the likes of you," he snarls.

We stand like statues as his face grows red.

"I said get, or this girl is going to pay!" He crushes Sadie tighter to his chest.

His cruelty makes me so angry everything looks red.

A scraping sound echoes on the cliff above me. I shift only my eyes, expecting Floyd. But it's a bighorn ram, gazing boldly into the valley.

Every eye is fixed on the ram's sudden appearance, and Mr. Carson whispers, "Recognize him?"

# -27-

I look closely and see the deep scratches on his huge horns. His fur still has marks from the imprisoning vines. I hold my breath as he leaps off the ledge, right over Mr. Carson and me. He lands with a poof of dust in the open space, and Packman shifts Sadie in the ram's direction.

"What's this now—some sort of trick? Get out of here, you varmint!" The man kicks a few stones at the ram. He leaps to the side, then shakes his huge head at Packman.

I look at Sadie, but her eyes are locked on the ram's. Packman's grip on her mouth loosens as he shifts, trying to keep Sadie between him and the ram.

She nods real slow, and I look back at the ram. He lifts his head, inspecting Sadie with one eye.

*He knows.*

One cloven hoof scrapes the ground. Packman is getting even more nervous; sweat is pouring down his neck. The ram tenses, sinking closer to the ground. Sadie nods one more time, and the ram launches forward at her signal. In three swift bounds, he's there. Sadie tucks her body, twisting hard to one side. The ram drops to his knees, skidding the last foot, then his horns slam into Packman. He and Sadie fly in different directions. Sadie curls in the air, then lands on her feet.

The ram rises high on his hind legs, paws the air, and aims his horns at Packman, who is flat on the ground. Then Floyd appears around a corner, his heavy features registering shock as the ram changes targets at the last second. Floyd slams into the cliff face behind him at the impact. He crumples into a limp pile, and the ram turns to us.

Ethan and I dare not move as the ram walks slowly up to Sadie. She holds out her hand; he won't quite let her touch his outstretched nose.

"Thanks, boy," she whispers. The ram dips his head, spins, and shoots away down the valley.

"Quick, boys! Grab those coils of rope and tie up those men!" Mr. Carson tries to rise but can't quite manage it.

Ethan and I leap into action. Packman is rolling on the ground, moaning and gripping his leg. Wrestling his arms behind his back and tying his wrists together doesn't bother me a bit. Then I pull Poppa's knife from his pocket and insert it back into my own.

Ethan has a harder time with Floyd, who is still as limp as a cooked noodle.

"Girl, help me up, will you?"

## Zion Gold Rush

Sadie rushes over, and with that surprising strength of hers, she gets him to his feet.

"You kids stay out here for a bit and keep an eye on these two." Mr. Carson limps slowly through the jumble of boulders and disappears into the mine.

I wrap Sadie in a hug. "Are you all right?" I ask, leaning back to study her face.

"He saved me!" she says with that spark I've been missing in her eyes. "And I'm all right now because I'm listening to the right voice again."

"Did you know what that ram was going to do?"

She grins. "It was like I could read his thoughts for a few seconds…as if he told me exactly what to do." I can tell she's thrilled with everything that's happened. Then she jabs Ethan with her elbow.

"Old Chiptomunkus Rex saved the day. Are you still archenemies?"

He sighs, with his hands resting on his narrow hips. "All is fair in love and war; at least that's what people say. I'm not sure I totally agree." He shrugs. "He earned a point, anyway."

"You are a tough nut to crack," she says.

"Yeah, don't get on my bad side; I'm like an elephant, and I never forget."

Mr. Carson limps out of the low entrance. He grimaces as he stands up straight. A loud pop echoes through the canyon, and he grabs his hip. "Oh, whoowee!" He stands up again, the pain leaving his face. "You know, I believe that pop put things to right." He walks our way with a far steadier gait.

"Boys, let's drag these ruffians around the corner. What do you say?"

I shrug, then take Packman by the shoulders. I ignore his shouts, but soon Mr. Carson pulls a handkerchief from his pocket and ties it around Packman's mouth. "I've heard about all I can take from you."

By the time we've gotten the men moved around the bend, I collapse on the ground.

"It's so hot," I murmur.

"Here, I've got some water."

## Zion Gold Rush

*It's good to have the real Sadie back.*

"What's that?" Ethan asks, pointing at a strange box in Mr. Carson's hand.

The old man shrugs. "I found it in the mine."

"Let me see it." Ethan takes it eagerly. "It's got a button on it."

The words hang in the air, and Mr. Carson shrugs. "It sure does."

Ethan studies it for a moment more, glances at us, then pushes the button.

## -28-

A blast of air hits me at the same time as the loudest sound I've ever heard seems to steal the breath right out of my lungs. The rumbling continues, rolling away through the canyon, and a thick plume of dust rises from around the bend.

Ethan uncovers his head. "Did I do that?"

We stare at each other until the dust settles.

"I reckon the rangers will be swarming around here soon. Then we won't have to drag these two lowlifes all the way back."

I squint at Mr. Carson. *Sure was strange that he'd gone back into the mine.* I creep forward and look around the bend. A huge pile of boulders is all

## Zion Gold Rush

that's left of the mine entrance. A smile curls one half of my mouth. Mr. Carson had set that dynamite and handed off the detonator to Ethan once he knew we would all be safe. *Now Zion's gold will forever remain a legend.*

I stare at the pile of rocks. I'm sort of glad for what he did. That gold mine sure didn't seem to do any good for the folks who had found it.

Sadie glides up next to me. "Why is your hair so glittery?"

I frown and run my hand through it. My fingers come out coated in gold dust. "They put that bag over my head!" I shake hard, and gold dust settles everywhere. "I guess that's all we'll ever see of Zion gold!"

"That's fine with me!" Sadie declares.

## -29-

"So," Dad wipes crumbs off his chest. "The rangers found the bags of gold that Floyd and Will had pulled out of the mine before Mr. Carson blew it. But they've decided to keep the whole incident a secret...or else this national park would need security guards 24/7. What an adventure y'all had while I was at work. What do you think about the code of silence they added to your Junior Ranger pledge?"

Sadie and I look at Ethan. The gold sure had gotten to him for a few minutes. I can't imagine what a mess it would make if the entire world knew gold was in Zion.

"I think it's the best decision." Then I stuff a

huge handful of popcorn into my mouth. It'd been a long hike already and so worth it.

"Nobody move!" Ethan says, so we freeze.

"Is it a rattler?" Mom asks.

"No. It's worse. It's Chiptomunkus Rex!"

I deflate and turn to find an army of chipmunks hurrying closer, and Rex is in the lead.

Ethan clutches his bag of popcorn to his chest. "Ha! I already ate my last duplex cookie! You can do nothing more to me, Chiptomunkus Rex!"

The big chipmunk with the dark spot on his head ignores Ethan entirely and, in a flash, he's sitting on Dad's knee.

"Well, you're a friendly little fellow, aren't you?" Dad says.

"Don't let his appearance fool you; he's a thief at heart," Ethan warns.

"Don't feed him, Dad! It's against park rules." Sadie's words halt Dad's hand holding a big popcorn kernel. Rex reaches up, pleading for it.

"Sorry, little guy." Dad pops it into his mouth.

Rex's beady little eyes squint, and I frown.

*Is he angry?*

Dad shifts, and the rental car keys peeking out of his pocket flash in the brilliant sunlight.

Rex dives onto them, pouncing at the light.

Dad flinches at the sudden move, the keys come loose, and chaos breaks out.

"I warned you he's a thief!" Ethan shouts, leaping for the big chipmunk with our car keys dangling from his mouth.

Rex dodges him easily, and Ethan lands with a hard bellyflop.

"NO!" Dad shouts, vaulting over Ethan. Dad misses too, and Rex dives for a hole as I swipe at his back leg. I stare at my empty hand.

"Oh, no," Mom says. We push and shove, all trying to look down the small dark tunnel in the rocks.

## Zion Gold Rush

"They're gone forever," Ethan whispers, then he throws back his head and cries, "I was wrong; there was more he could do to me!"

Dad puts his head in his hands for a minute, then mutters, "I may as well get it over with."

He pulls out his phone. "Hello, yes, I'm sure you get this all the time, but I need to report a small issue with the car I rented from your company. A chipmunk stole the keys."

He's silent for a moment.

"No, I'm serious; a chipmunk stole the keys."

Minutes later, he hangs up with his face red. "Well, that was an interesting conversation."